CELIA'S HEAVEN

Nancy Canyon

CELIA'S HEAVEN

Nancy Canyon

Penchant Press International, LLC
Blaine, Washington
United States of America

Penchant Press International, LLC
P.O. Box 1333
Blaine, WA 98231
penchantpressinternational.com

Nancy Canyon 1951-

Celia's Heaven Nancy Canyon
ISBN 978-0-9998048-3-4
LCCN 2019956579

Cover design by: spokendesigns.com
Cover art by: Nancy Canyon

For my sister, Loretta

CHAPTER ONE

Celia knew it wouldn't be long before the lake froze over. The weather forecaster predicted an early snowfall, feet of the white stuff burying Vinegar Valley for weeks and weeks on end. Once the valley was blanketed, there'd be no chance to see Star walking along the silent shore, no chance to hear her angelic voice once again, but tonight, on the anniversary of her death, she could rise again. Celia believed this to be true, so she stood at the north end of Lake Monroe, waiting for Star to appear as a ripple of light or a wind-ruffle stirring the lake's surface. Perhaps the giant lilies would whisper and lift as Star rose from the chilly depths, appearing in a scintilla of light or an icy vapor above the water.

"Star," Celia called, peering through the dusky light, raising her voice to cry out again. "Star!" The sound of her voice muffled beneath the cloud-thickened sky. She listened hard. Nothing. About to turn and walk away, she saw a movement—near a giant lily pad, the surface swelled enough for rings to spread across it, moving toward where she waited on the shore.

Celia stood motionless. Seconds passed and the water smoothed again. She searched the upturned leaves, the withering snarls, the sunken masses. A gust of icy wind lifted her inky hair off the nape of her neck. She shuddered, pulling her hood over her head and buttoning her coat at the throat, swallowing into the tightness that had been bothering her all day. Would she ever be free of her bone pain—or had it worked its way so deeply into her cells that people mistook her shadowed eyes for the jezebel her daddy promised she was, rather than the grief-stricken girl she was at heart.

Celia read that twins were symbiotically connected and that it was natural for their spirits to remain close, even if one died before the other. Wearing Star's brown boots kept Celia connected, steadying her as she stepped over root tangles and scurried up moldering rises as effortlessly as she moved on a man.

A twig snapped and she flicked her penlight in the direction of the sound. Holding her breath, she searched the shadowy woods for an intruder, but nothing stirred in the forest's tangle of limbs but her own skittering heart.

Jay was always saying to her, "The woods are too dangerous at night. I'll drive you to the Toi Toy Club."

She always replied, "I'll be fine, JJ. Don't worry about me, please!"

She worked around men and knew when they meant harm. She could smell it on them. Mostly they were starved for love like everyone else. Besides, her best friend Raven (a former MP) had taught her protective maneuvers, like twisting a man's hand away from his body until he dropped to his knees. Raven always said, "*Easy as pie, Sugar,*" and then pretend demonstrated her favorite move—bending a finger back until it nearly snapped in two. *They'll go down. You'll see.* She hoped she'd never have to try it out on someone.

Now, in the dusky light, Celia recalled Grandpa Monroe's story about the fruit picker who'd wandered into the orchard late one night to steal apples for his family. That man disappeared. Her grandmother's hands worried her apron when Grandpa talked about "disappearances," as it wasn't the only time someone had wandered onto their property and was never seen nor heard from again. Celia and Star were ordered to watch out for each other and stay away from the fence on the far side of the lake where a hidden road cut east through to the firing range. Grandpa shook his head and said, "Mere twists of rusty barbwire won't stop a perv."

The stories gave Celia childish nightmares. She recalled the time she'd awakened from a bad dream with her heart pounding in her chest. Star slept beside her, moonlight streaming through the attic window, lighting her sister's pale locks like candlelight on the churchhouse altar. The sight comforted Celia. Soon she had fallen back asleep again. But then there were the other nights, like when she lay awake recalling her mother comparing Star's hair to spider silk. They'd been walking around the lake, taking in the sunshine and the scent of yellow flag irises. Celia held a stalk of velvety cattail in her hand. She'd said, "What about me, Mama? What about *my* hair?"

Her mother's eyes darkened. "Your curls are as black and tangled as lily roots," she said.

The memory still haunted Celia. Maybe it wasn't just her curls that were black and tangled. Didn't the men who told her she was beautiful, the ones she was always tempted to bring back home while Jay was working dog shift, disprove her mother's assessment? She couldn't put a finger on the reason she'd gone the way she'd gone, but she knew it wasn't because of the color of her hair.

Celia turned from the lake and followed the path—her usual route to work–past withering tules, turning northeast at the far end of the lake where the trail wound past the orchard and disappeared into the woods. She hadn't lost hope that she'd hear from her twin one last time. As she stepped carefully through the dusky light, she pondered the Monroe Miracle. Her grandfather drowned and resurrected—a well-known story in Vinegar Valley, though many of the witnesses were now long gone. Her grandfather, if he were alive still, would have agreed that receiving a message from Celia's deceased twin was entirely possible.

Celia stepped out of the woods onto Orchard Street. She walked between Raven's Mustang and Dan's Ford pickup and headed up the stairs to the porch smelling of piss and beer. Star hadn't received the Monroe Miracle, which troubled Celia. Was it just the men who miraculously healed? Scoffing, she studied the bits of scrap paper, thumbtacks, and staples littering the wall around her poster: *Now Starring at the Toi Toy Club, Celia Monroe*. Her heavily made-up eyes gazed luridly down from the glossy paper. She knew how the townsfolk felt about her stripping; her daddy had made that clear enough. Always, she argued with him that his parishioners could only know what she was doing if they too had been in the audience. She drew her hand over the curling poster and tacked the perforated corner down, mouthing, "Come and get it, bad boys." Perhaps she should be embarrassed for herself, but she wasn't. After all, she was very well paid for her *dark and tangled* nature.

When she first started stripping at Dan's establishment, rock and roll rattled the club's tinderbox walls. Two years later, it continued to stir her sensually, although the smell of the place grossed her out. She shrugged her shoulders, realizing the growing stink wouldn't kill her and if the secondhand smoke did, she'd be floating next to Star in Heaven (if there was such a place) all that much sooner.

Grateful for the empty hall, she hurried along, hoping she'd make it to the tanning room before Heckelman cornered her. Just the other night while buckling her stilettos, he'd come up behind her and smacked her on the ass. She'd wheeled around and slapped his face. "Prick," she'd said, and hurried off.

"Don't even think about skipping out," he'd yelled after her. "Men need what they need. That's why you're here." Then he doubled over with one of his coughing fits.

Anticipating the heat of sunlamps cooking her chilly skin, she picked up her pace. Tanning was the only perk she received besides beer and wine, and she looked forward to baking beneath the light before each rehearsal began. Heat relaxed and limbered her body—lessening her bone pain a bit. As she passed the lunchroom, Dan wheeled around the corner, dressed in his usual attire: sneakers and jeans and a black silk shirt open at the neck.

"Late again," he said, and tossed down what was left of his smoke. He scuffed it out with the toe of a tennis shoe. "What's with the big eyes?" he said, leaning in too close. "You know you're a flake."

"I'm early," Celia said, attempting to push past him, but he blocked her way with his arm. "Move," she said. "I've just enough time to work on my tan before rehearsal."

Before Dan could reply, he erupted in lung-rattling hacks. Celia stepped back, repulsed by his spasms, a reminder of the time she'd seen him stomping around outside the bail bonds building like a spoiled child. She'd looked at him askance ever since—wondering what he was up to. Despite her feelings of disgust, she couldn't keep from staring at the gold chain nestled in the reddish hair of his chest.

He continued to sputter as he pulled a crumpled pack of Camels from his pocket. "What're you staring at?" he said, lighting up.

"Nothing!" She nodded toward the entrance. "You better fix that sign. With all those burnt bulbs, the sign reads Toity Club. Your joint's in the toilet."

"With a sexy starlet like you—never." Dan exhaled smoke, stepping closer to flick the neck of Celia's buttoned-up coat. He grinned. "On your way to church, goodie girl?"

"You know I'm with Jay." She started off again, but Dan grabbed her wrist and pulled her back.

"Forget the fuckup, baby," he said, leaning close. "We're good together. You and me!"

"You're an asshole." She held her breath against the smell of Brut and nicotine. "There is no *us*!" She twisted his hand, breaking his grip on her arm, leaving him grousing as she hurried off down the hall.

Celia slammed the tanning room door and collapsed against its flimsy veneer. She didn't want to fight with Dan, or anyone else, for that matter. She shrugged off her winter coat and collapsed into the folding chair. Her heart pounded as she rummaged through her purse. The contents hadn't contained a cigarette for over six months. Growling, she threw the purse on the floor. She could always bum one off her boss, but decided to avoid another encounter with the fuckhead, if at all possible.

Celia switched on the row of silver sunlamps and stripped off her clothes. The timer ticked as she flapped out a fresh towel, covering the stained chaise. She relaxed back, soaking in the heat. As it warmed her skin, the smell of Dan's Brut wafted from her wrist into the stale air. The smell brought with it a sick feeling, the same feeling that had come over her last month when some sleazy guy left the club, his zipper hanging open from a lap dance taken too far. She had stepped into the shadows and waited for him to pass.

In some ways, she hated them all, in other ways, she couldn't get enough of her customers. Always, with the right size bill offered and a seductive smile purred, she could ignore being called *sweetcakes* and step into any stranger's arms, except for that guy. He was even too sleazy for her.

For some reason, she was hornier than ever that particular night. After *fly-open-guy* drove off, she walked back inside and looked around for someone to buy her a drink. The bar was empty except for a few frogs. She slipped down the hall to Dan's office and moved silently behind him, drawing cool fingers down the nape of his neck. He lurched around, looking startled. Taking him home with her the night the hole in her middle had grown so voluminous that the whole valley could fit inside—trees, lakes, mountains, even the firing range—had been one of her bigger mistakes.

Clearing her mind of the memory, she focused on the heat penetrating her body. Soon, where there had been goose-bumps rippling her arms and legs, her skin glistened pink. Her breathing settled into a regular rhythm and despite the hollow thumping of Dan's funky sound system vibrating thin walls, Celia drifted, her fingers relaxing over the scar tissue pocking her upper thighs. The texture faded from her consciousness as she floated into a dream, sinking to the bottom of the lake to rest in its murkiness, her hair undulating like snakes coiling around her head, her breath rising through the green water in bubbles rupturing across the surface. Star swam toward her, gliding out of the murkiness, her strong limbs propelling her forward, her golden hair fanning around her face, bubbles trailing off her arms as they glided toward each other. Celia reached out, anticipating Star's vibrant fingers with an urgen-cy that only the sleeping know. Like willowy weeds, their bodies floated in the current, hands twining together, feet moving in lazy kicks. They smiled, fingers outlining each oth-er's faces. Then a splash and they both turned to see bottom muck stirring up around the roots of the giant lilies. From the past, Vanessa's words came ringing back to Celia: "There, see? It's just as I said, the lake monster. That's why you must stay close to shore."

"Don't worry," Star whispered, ignoring their mother's warning, her mouth close to Celia's ear. "I'll take care of you," she said, pulling Celia toward the surface.

Celia looked around, trying to see through the silt stream-ing around them. She gasped, crossing her arms over her naked breasts, startling herself awake to gulp musty air.

"Someone's watching," she said, bolting upright through the bright light of the sunlamp. Her heart kept beat with the ticking timer. Gasping, she worked to catch her breath.

After Star's funeral, the blackness in her middle grew larger. Summer no longer held joy for her. She recalled standing in front of the woodstove on a scorching hot summer day, burning the funeral program her mama had put in her hand. She held the twist of flaming paper to the tip of a Winston. It only took one puff to screw her head sideways and turn her legs to pudding; and down she went into the rocker, the cigarette dangling between her fingers. She watched through her nicotine stupor as the curl of smoke rose toward the ceiling. When the cigarette dropped onto her exposed thigh, it seared her tender skin. The sting snapped her to attention. She was surprised to find that the pain didn't sicken her; in fact, each pull of her clothing across the angry burn lessened her gloom a tiny bit.

After that night, every time grief drew her close to the bone, she'd hold the glowing ash up to the skin of her thigh until her heart thrummed like helicopter blades. It was the flush of warmth, a feeling similar to the rush of an orgasm that she began to depend upon to calm her nerves. That is, until after a performance one evening when Raven walked in just as Celia was about to press the glowing cigarette against her bare skin.

Raven shouted, "Stop that, girl," and grabbed the smoke out of her hand. Raven rubbed out the Winston with the toe of her spike-heeled shoe. As she dabbed cold cream on Celia's wounds, she explained how vets were taught to deal with flashbacks. They counted backwards while visualizing a safe place in nature. "That's right, Sugar. Better deal with what's eatin' at you."

After that, Celia actually tried visualizing the place by the lake where she liked to stretch out on a blanket in the sun, but when she missed Star so deeply that several glasses of wine didn't dent her bone pain, she gave in, lit up, and lowered her jeans.

Celia jumped at the loud knock. "Ceal, you in there?"

"I'm here, Raven," she said, slipping the flat of her hand over her bare skin, feeling the quickened thump of her heart beneath her fingertips.

"Bindi and Kiko's AWOL. It's just you and me, Sugar," Raven said. "Hurry up. We got rehearsin' to do."

Celia slipped on Star's boots, wrapped herself in a towel, and hurried across the hall to the dressing room. From the contents of her locker she pulled tiny bits of material she called *a costume*. Digging further, she felt around for the pint of whiskey she remembered hiding under the mess of clothes and spike heels piled at the bottom of the locker. She found nothing but an empty bottle and a crumpled Winston pack, which she tossed back into the mess. "Dammit!"

Dropping the towel to the floor, she pulled on a feathered G-string and pasted on black nipple tassels. Bending forward, she positioned her breasts inside the red sequined bra that she'd remove later. She checked her reflection in the mirror, plumping herself a little more on the left, and feeling satisfied, walked away from the mirror in search of a shot of whiskey and a cigarette.

Celia'd promised Dan she wouldn't drink before going on stage, but tonight was different. She'd fallen off the wagon so many times that the damn thing had gotten tossed in the rusty heap behind the boathouse, along with bedsprings, tire rims, and old fishing nets. Someday, maybe she'll get clean, but not tonight; not on the anniversary of Star's death.

The ceiling tiles creaked as the Toi Toy Club expanded with a huff of wind; as it exhaled, all the air seemed to be drawn from the room. Clicking, steady and even, came from everywhere and nowhere at the same time. Gasping, Celia felt sick to her stomach. She knew there'd never been a tornado in Vinegar Valley, but somehow the sigh of the building reminded her of a coming storm.

Calming herself, she leaned close to the mirror to glue on false eyelashes, knocking over the photo the preacher had taken of the twins on their seventeenth birthday. She set the photo upright again with shaky hands. It was a good picture of Celia, with her skin all bronzed from swimming in the lake, her dark eyes penetrating, yet wary. And Star…it was almost as if Celia could hear her sister's sweet voice speaking to her from the photo, "Love you, Ceal." Celia looked around the room. "Sissy?" she gasped.

Another snap and what sounded like footsteps in the hall had her hands shaking even harder. Celia dropped the eyelash glue applicator on the counter. Clear fluid puddled from its pointed tip. "Shit!" She wiped up the spill with a Kleenex then turned from the mirror, calling out, "Raven? Is that you?"

Celia listened, but there was no answer. She pulled on her robe and soundlessly stepped toward the door. Sticking her head out, she looked up and down the empty hall. The flickering, humming fluorescents that she'd complained to Dan about more than once, made her shiver. Unsettled, she turned back to the dressing room, trying to ignore the raised hair at the nape of her neck.

The twins had always been a little tetched—that's what their grandmother called seeing and hearing things. Star could be trying to get her attention from beyond the veil. She'd seen the water change earlier, no one could tell her otherwise. She looked up at the ceiling, taking in the space above the row of lockers. She listened for the knocking sound. All was silent. She turned back to the mirror to finish her makeup.

Celia remembered how once on the way home from school, Star had bolted off. She followed her to the outcrop of basalt overlooking the military firing range. She'd stood waiting in the fall heat, her books growing heavier by the minute. It wasn't the first time Star had run off. It seemed like Celia was always waiting for her sister and on that particular day, being famished and fatigued from school, all she wanted was to get home for a slice of her mama's homemade bread. Finally, bored and irritated, she'd dropped onto a rock and picked at the scab on her knee, calling out every few minutes, "Star? Star?"

Growing sleepy, she closed her eyes. She daydreamed that Star was speaking to a wolf. Her twin scratched him beneath his chin and shook his paw like she did with their grandfather's dog. Suddenly, the wolf turned and faced Celia, staring directly into her eyes. The animal licked her face and Celia's eyes jerked open. Star was standing in front of her, radiant in the afternoon sunlight. "Come on," she said. "Let's go."

A door slammed. Celia jumped. "Fuck the spooks," she whispered. She took up a pencil and finished lining her eyes with kohl. She blinked, smudging the kohl at the corners. Feeling satisfied that her makeup was complete, she stood before the mirror, her hips swinging, making lazy eights to an imaginary song. She saw nothing behind her or to her sides; no shadow, no haze, no spark of light. Nor did she feel the icy cold air that meant a ghost was present. She drew a hand evocatively down her belly, darkening her gaze. Liquid-like, she snaked her arms above her head and leaned backwards in a sultry bend. She curved lower, facing an upside-down view of the dressing room, which now included a statuesque figure towering in the doorway. Abruptly, Celia righted herself. "Raven? You scared the bejesus out of me. I thought I heard you coming down the hall earlier."

"Weren't me, Sugar. I was chattin' with that new bartender, William. Beau-ti-ful." Raven gave Celia a wink as she spun on her spikes and slapped her ass. Black as a burnt match and shining with baby oil, she was a high-strung racehorse with twitching muscles and prancing feet. "It's gonna be a blast dancin' for Star tonight. You'll see," she laughed.

"Celia smiled. Seems like just yesterday that Star and I raced each other to the water lilies and back." She lowered her head. "Oh man, she sure loved the water."

"Sugar, you got to let her go," Raven said, gathering Celia into her big arms.

"I feel like half a person without her."

Raven hugged Celia tightly. "You ain't identical, girl. You're from two different yolks."

"I know what we are," Celia said, pushing Raven away. "But we were mashed together for nine months, you know. Believe me, we're the same as identical."

"You were roommates, that's all." Raven turned at the sound of Dan's footsteps. "Shit, where *are* the others? We still got rehearsin' to do."

Dan slapped the dressing room door as he passed. "Move it, Dolls. Hour and counting…."

Raven and Celia paraded into the dingy lounge smelling of left-over smoke and sour booze. As they crossed the frayed rug, the side door slammed open and three exotic dancers practically toppled in, laughing and stumbling drunk.

"You're late," Dan shouted from the lighted platform above. He switched the lights from red to blue to purple in a frenzied manner.

"What the hell," Donna said, brushing him off with a wave of her hand. She pinched Kiko's ass as they sauntered toward the stage. Petite Kiko shrieked and pinched Donna back. Then the two of them gave Bindi a playful shove. Bindi tripped, then caught herself on a chair back. Recovering, she did a mock burlesque routine, swinging a leg over the chair back and tipping her imaginary hat. The others joined sexily. From the stage, Raven laughed hyena-like, her big black hand coming up to cover her wide-open mouth.

Dan banged on the platform. "Get to work, bitches," he yelled, swinging his arms like a crazy man, "or I'll can every goddamned one of your shapely asses."

Everyone scrambled onto stage except for Celia, who flopped into a chair to watch her friends twirling around poles, flipping upside down and spinning to the floor, toes pointing through the flood of purple light in arabesques, the smalls of their backs arching suggestively, their splits wider than imaginable, their attitude seductively sultry.

All this for Star, Celia thought. The wind breathed the building again and for a moment, Celia imagined she could smell violets. Tingles crawled up her arms and across her bare shoulders. She looked around, feeling the energy sparkle, the same energy she used to feel when Star was about to walk into a room. She knew the two of them were magnets attracted to each other, even with Star now residing in the afterlife.

She remembered sitting beneath an apple tree once, eating fermented fallen fruit until the twins hiccupped and giggled like drunken GIs. Soon, they were rolling around on the ground laughing until Daddy showed up and ordered them back to work. They hauled handfuls of twigs to the fire that he'd been attending, the two of them staggering between trees until the alcohol had them curled together, sleeping it off beneath a fat apple branch at the back of the orchard.

Celia anticipated Bindi's backbend and ran a hand down her own thigh as if she were doing the move herself. She felt the burn scars and the little bit of joy she'd been experiencing vanished. She jumped from her chair and despite the precarious stilettos she wore, bolted from the lounge, and down the hall into the dressing room.

Banging open her locker, she located an old clutch at the bottom of the mess and ripped open the pocket. "Damn! Still no smokes." She dropped into a chair and scratched her thighs until the scars welted with red nail marks. "Why didn't the Monroe Miracle resurrect Star? The men in the family had been healed—goddamn them anyway! It's always the men!"

Just last week Daddy'd cut wood into stove-length pieces and slung them onto the porch. He'd been doing this ever since she could remember and still he repeated the story when finished: *The axe flipped from my hand, nearly severing my toe. Blood gushed everywhere.*

Celia lifted her foot onto the chair and began applying the thick makeup she used to cover her burn scars. She wept as she worked, seeing in her mind's eye her sister's dead body at the funeral. She looked peaceful enough—her perfect body tucked inside the casket. Her hair gleamed like spun gold, and her skin blushed with the makeup the funeral home had applied sweetly.

"Then it happened," Daddy would say with wide misty eyes. "God's love healed me. Not a scratch left on my toe. I too had been blessed with the Monroe Miracle."

Ticking sounds crossed the ceiling. Celia looked up just as Raven ducked into the dressing room. "Come on Sugar, it's showtime."

CHAPTER TWO

It was Sunday morning and while the preacher was giving his sermon, Celia sat on the edge of a cot in a remote room in Luna Sanitarium's west wing. She was tired from working the night before, headachy, and grumpy that her mother had ended up in the coldest chamber at the end of the longest hall in the hospital. While Celia waited for the nurse to finish her duties, she studied the cots lining the far wall, imagining crazy ghosts, sleepless in the night, climbing out of their beds to roam the halls in their nightgowns and PJs. Surely there were more friendly rooms in this voluminous hospital, maybe even ones with companionable patients—sane ones that is—who could keep her mother company until Vanessa snapped out of shock and returned home.

Seeing Vanessa's reed-like body backlit against the tall winter windows filled Celia with a grave heaviness. The nurse left the room and Celia rose from the cot and approached her mother's wheelchair.

"Hi Mama," she said, and pulled a chair up in front of her. She tucked the white blanket around Vanessa's legs and arranged her hands like frosty stems, fingers curling upward in her thin lap. "The doctor says you'll come back to us soon, Mama. Won't it be nice to sleep in your own bed again? Sit at the kitchen table and sip black tea?"

Celia pushed her mother's graying hair away from her face. Vanessa's dark eyes were unresponsive. Celia recalled a Sunday long ago when the preacher leaned over his wife and kissed first one cheek, then the other. He was dressed in black, flourishing his hands like he did while anointing his baptismal sheep in the little churchhouse sanctuary.

Celia frowned when she thought of her daddy visiting her mama. He rarely came to visit, that was the whole of it. *Doesn't he care about her?* Celia looked around the room. Against the south wall sat a dresser filled with Vanessa's underwear and nightgowns. The piece of furniture reminded Celia of the antique dresser she kept in her old attic bedroom. Once, when Sunday service was still being held in the little churchhouse, she caught her daddy pawing through the top drawer during coffee hour. When she walked in, she asked him what he was doing. He said, "Just looking for your mother's…" and brushed Celia aside as he hurried downstairs to the kitchen to hide amongst the yammering parishioners. Celia'd yelled after him, "Stay out of my things," but he dismissed her with a wave of his hand, saying something about her being crazy, just like her mother. After he left, her stomach sickened as she straightened her silky underthings. It creeped her out; he'd been fondling her underwear.

At times Celia found herself arguing with the preacher, going on in her mind about his lack of trust in her. She took a deep breath and closed her eyes, sitting in the hard wooden chair in the big room. When she opened them again, the clouds outside the sanitarium had thinned, letting wispy light through the windows, brightening and elongating their shadows across the floor until they resembled small coffins. She looked away, distracting herself by stroking her mother's hands. Her mother was not going to die!

"Mama," Celia said. "I need your help. I'm thinking it's time we set Star free. Her ashes have been sitting in the back of my closet for over a year now."

Vanessa's brown eyes remained downturned. She didn't answer. She never answered.

"Talk to me, Mama. Please."

Celia sighed, dropping her head into her hands. The smell of Pine-Sol made her feel ill. Why didn't they use a sweet scent to clean the place? *Violets*, she thought. She shook her head. It hurt. Why'd she have to party after practice last night, guzzling down beer with the other dancers? Raven warned her to be careful, but when she was sad, she lost control more easily than she liked. Her friend drove her home and poured her into her bed. Daddy was right: she was the lush he promised she was.

Celia leaned close to her mother. "Anyway, I think Star'd prefer her ashes be scattered in the lake, don't you?" She held her breath, studying the nightstand where a bowl of uneaten pudding congealed. A taut skin formed over the dessert making Celia think of jizz and the last time she and JJ had been together. She thought of his warm hands drawing down her sides. She'd be ready for him tonight.

"Well, I better get going," Celia said, standing to pull on her coat. "I'm making dinner for Jay. Chicken cacciatore, with a jar of tomato sauce from the fruit cellar—the sauce you canned yourself, remember?"

The sun broke through the clouds for a moment, brightening the casket shapes across the floor. Celia leaned in to kiss her mother's cheek. "You don't have to answer me just yet," she said. "Just think about it. Maybe next time you'll have an answer for me."

As Celia careened along Luna Lake Road, she thought of different ways she could wake her mother—loud music and a striptease would surely do it. She laughed aloud as she imagined the doctor walking in unexpectedly, as he often did. He was nice enough, but sometimes looked at her with an exasperated expression. Once he said, "You can't hurry a shock victim. You'll have to wait, just like the rest of us." It was after that look that she began giving him her best irritated look. It was after that look that he reminded her that the Monroe family was behind on their bill.

She sucked her teeth as she drove, speeding around curves. At the bottom of Luna Hill, Celia slowed the Chevy and turned right onto the highway. Ahead, a military convoy traveled south toward Firing Range Road. Stepping on the gas, Celia sped ahead, hoping to catch up with the string of jeeps. She liked making eyes at the GIs.

War practice at the firing range had left the townsfolk with erratic ticks and bitten nails. Even Celia had developed a habit of anticipating explosions, tightening her neck and back, and when nothing happened, letting out an irritated sigh. As for the army preparing its troops for Nam, she'd like to give them a piece of her mind—all those explosives shaking dust down from the rafters, motes sifting through hot attic air, coating rugs and trunks and cotton bedspreads throughout the valley. And why continue bombing practice when the war was coming to an end? "By God, just knock it the fuck off!"

Star's belongings were peppered with crumbled chinking. Someday Celia would haul everything to the dump, that is, once she felt emotionally ready to climb the squeaky stairs without her bone pain pricking her like Alabaster's claws. She shrugged her shoulders as she edged to the center line, and then, flooring it, encouraged her rusty Chevy to overtake one jeep after another. She smiled, tossing her hair for GIs who might recognize her the next time they visited the club. *Maybe they'll leave extra big tips*, she thought. Or *tits* as the GIs liked to say, laughing it up with big knee-slapping guffaws—*Here's your big tit*, they'd smirk, stuffing the money into her bra.

Part of her wanted to slap them silly; the other part of her wanted to keep them happy, after all, they were paying her bills. She swerved to the front of the line, waving in her rear-view mirror as she barreled down Route 1, heading for the Pay 'n Go's parking lot where she'd stock up on wine and groceries for the following week.

CHAPTER THREE

It was early Sunday afternoon by the time the preacher climbed in his truck, ready to stop by the little churchhouse for his weekly visit with Celia. Things had been topsy-turvy at his church that morning and now he was back at home, running late with a vehicle that wouldn't start parked out front. He telephoned his daughter. "Celia?"

"Who else would it be?" Celia snapped.

"Okay, okay," he said, feeling resigned already by her angry resistance. "My truck just conked out. I need you to come pick me up."

"No can do. I'm fixing dinner," she said. "It's a special night for Jay and me, you know."

Ed thought about the cheese and crackers and cup of hot tea Celia always had waiting for him. His mouth watered and for a moment he imagined he was sitting in his daughter's kitchen at the picnic table. He pictured her leaning over the phone, one hip jutted sideways in those tight jeans she always wore. As usual, her blouse would be open one button too low at the neck. And she'd be flirting with that cop boyfriend of hers; so lascivious, that dark daughter of his.

"Daddy?"

"What?" he said, focusing on his kitchen table with its clutter of dirty mugs he needed to wash and put away. He'd let things go since he'd moved Vanessa into the sanitarium. Etta helped him on occasion, but he couldn't ask her all the time for housekeeping favors. He muttered into the receiver, "Oh, okay, I'll find a ride then. I'll see you soon."

"Whatever, but don't be long. I have to get dinner started."

"Eh huh," the preacher said, and hung up the receiver. He looked through his address book for Etta's phone number.

It's the booze that makes Celia so obstinate, he thought. The Devil lived in that girl and if Ed did anything right during his pitiful life, it would be to give her a chance to redeem herself—take away the drink and that vulgar stripping job, point her soul toward purity and light. *That's what fathers are for*, he thought. "That's what preachers are for," he said. But Celia was a tough nut to crack. She hardly ever said *yes*. He nodded, hearing her voice in his head saying, "No way, José!" And, "No, I won't drive you to see Mama. No, I won't pick up your groceries. No, I won't help you winterize the church." *She's like a two-year-old.*

Ed knew there were a number of reasons a daughter should obey her father. Number one was the obeisance to God's laws. Number two, he still owned the little churchhouse—she was getting a free ride living there.

Celia slammed down the telephone receiver, shaking her head at her daddy's expectations. "What next? Fix his truck?" she said, putting away groceries.

She finished up in the kitchen and revived the fire with a few sticks of wood. It snapped and popped cheerily as she set the teakettle on the stove. The preacher loved Lipton and cheddar on saltines. She made enough for Jay and set the plate of snacks on the picnic table.

She dressed down, jeans and a T-shirt, so Daddy wouldn't give her hell. Maybe she should give *him* hell for fidgeting with the hem of his coat, rubbing the oblong buttons, the corduroy patches on his elbows, touching the Bible he always carried beneath his arm, worrying the ring that was now slightly embedded into his fleshy finger, like fence wire choking an old apple tree.

Celia sat down at the table with a glass of wine and opened the Fanny Farmer's Cookbook. Daddy complained about her drinking, said it was a problem, but really it wasn't much—just a few glasses of rosé a night. She could still dance after three drinks, so what was the big fucking deal? Even Dan gave her shit. Who wants to be ragged on constantly? Her life was hers, wasn't it? Besides, the alcohol buzz felt good, euphoric even, heady like the smell of heavy perfume on a hot summer night.

It was three o'clock by the time she stood at the kitchen counter, unwrapping the pale bird with the thin skin dimpled with a smattering of pinfeathers. She would follow the instructions, using the ingredients Jay loved: garlic, oregano, tomato sauce, parmesan cheese, and so forth. *Click, click, click.*

She turned to the open window, thinking this time, the sound was coming from outside. Sometimes it came from behind the stove. At times, it came from the ceiling above the kitchen table. The sky was darkening beyond the valley. The wind gusted. *Click, click, click.* She shrugged, pulling the drumstick away from the bird. "Ready for the hatchet?"

Celia rocked the tip of the knife between pink joints, doing the best she could to sever thigh from leg and breast from back. Meat made her squeamish, but Jay's carnivorous appetite was hearty. She wanted to please him. Most of the time, anyway. Watching him dab up sauce with bread and wash it down with red wine encouraged the little bit of domesticity she managed to muster. *It rewards his waistline*, she thought, setting the chicken aside while she mixed flour with salt and pepper for breading. *And love handles.* She'd suggested he use a little restraint. He just grinned and took another bite.

Celia was only occasionally willing to go to such efforts to please his palette. Mostly she enjoyed petting the cat while eating peanut butter on saltines and drinking wine by the fire. It was important for a dancer to keep her waistline slim. A noon meal would make her belly pooch by the time she stripped that evening—so she ate nothing after a breakfast of toast and coffee. Raven once said, "Extra flesh, Sugar, keeps you from floatin' off to Heaven." But she wasn't stick thin; in fact, Celia saw herself as voluptuous, with tumbling breasts and sassy hips that took up a goodly amount of space in any man's imagination.

She dredged the chicken pieces in white flour and dropped them into sizzling butter to brown, and for the moment delighted in being domestic. When she had a bad encounter with a pushy club customer, life unfolding with sit-down meals and regular bedtimes for children seemed promising. "Children!"

she laughed, dropping the last two pieces of chicken into the pan, splatting her bare arm with hot fat. "Ouch! Who am I kidding? They'd starve to death with me as their mother!"

Her cat twined between her legs. She turned to Alabaster. "Where'd I put that roasting pan?" she said.

She knelt next to the stove and reached to the back of the cupboard, pawing through salt and pepper shakers, napkin holders, stacks of plastic plates and bowls, pie tins, and buffet sundries once used for churchhouse picnics and Sunday coffee hours. She couldn't find the roasting pan, so dropped onto her hands and knees and crawled partway inside the dark cupboard, reaching into the far back corner. "Ooh! Alabaster, it stinks like mice in here."

Alabaster rubbed against her thigh. "Kitty, kitty. There's a mouse in the house," she said, her hand touching the roasting pan at last. She began backing out of the cupboard just as a loud *whoooomp* brought her head up under the cupboard frame with enough force to cause her to see stars. She heard Alabaster's skidding claws on the linoleum, rounding the corner to the bedroom as she fell backwards onto the floor. "Fuck!" she said, holding her head in her hands. Two more explosions rattled the windows. She imagined mortars flying hillsides of dirt into the air, readying the troops for bloody mutilations in Nam. "Goddamned war practice!"

She touched the rising welt with light pressure causing her eyes to water, her mascara to streak. The chicken began to burn. She leaned up on her elbow, reached for the knob on the front of the stove and turned it off. "Fuck war," she said, lying back on the floor again. Alabaster crept around the corner, padding over to sniff her lips. "Yes, I'm alive. Unfortunately." She stroked the cat, remembering how the creepy lieutenant from the base had told her it wouldn't be long now before they pulled out of Nam. She shivered, recalling the evening they'd met at a restaurant on the outskirts of town. There were explosions that night too, accompanied by canned music and the smell of bathroom deodorizer. She felt exposed sitting there in the nearly empty restaurant.

At one point, he'd leaned in and said, "I'm married. Do you mind?"

"Of course not," she'd said. "We're just enjoying dinner together, right?"

"Not exactly," he'd said, closing his menu, raising his eyebrows. He leaned across the table and took her hand, squeezing it a little too hard. A shiver of fear fluttered down the nape of her neck.

"I think I'll have the chicken cacciatore," she said, and jerked her hand away. She got up from the table. "If you'll excuse me, I'd like to freshen up a bit." She grabbed her purse, walked down the hall, and slipped out the back door.

Several months later Raven slammed a folded newspaper down on the makeup counter in front of Celia and said, "See, Sugar? That's what I'm sayin'. Be careful."

Celia skimmed the article, then looked up, staring into Raven's worried eyes. Trent was in the brig for beating his wife's head in. When Celia'd looked more closely at the picture, she realized it was taken in the same restaurant that served JJ's favorite dish. She was glad she'd followed her intuition that night and skipped out on the creep.

Celia rolled onto her side and sat up. She pushed herself to standing, steadying herself at the kitchen stove. Even though she felt weak, she managed to transfer the blackened chicken from frying pan into the dented roaster. She poured her mother's canned marinara over the meat and hefted the pan into the oven. Alabaster continued to twine between her ankles as she worked. "It's okay, baby," she said, and tossed him a scrap of scorched skin. He licked it delicately. "I burnt the heck out of it, sorry," she said, refilling her glass with rosé. Feeling exhausted, she dropped into the rocker next to the fire.

Vanessa was frying up two hens the very day she lapsed to stone. Celia figured it was the comment she'd made about Star's love of chicken wings that had pushed their mother over the edge. As she rocked, she watched the sky grow inky. That terrible day she'd sat in the passenger seat of Daddy's truck, her mother wedged between them. Celia faced the truck window, tears blurring the currant bushes to dusty smears as they bumped up the hill to Luna Sanitarium. Neither she nor her daddy spoke as they wound past Luna Lake. Staring at the reflection in the side mirror, she'd watched the tiny lake resting passively at the bottom of the hospital grounds. It was rumored that one of the crazies had drowned in Luna Lake on a hot summer evening. The orderlies didn't find her for several days, and when they did, they looked at their shoes when recalling her mermaid crayon drawings pinned to the wall of the activity room.

The preacher's voice bellowed over the engine noise, startling Celia. He suggested Luna Sanitarium might serve as a cure-all for her need to embarrass the Monroe family before all of Vinegar Valley. Over the engine noise he said something about her unchristian behavior being the ruin of the Monroe's good name.

Celia sipped her wine. She was feeling riled and soon found herself gritting her teeth as she imagined herself leaping across the truck seat that day and choking her daddy until he fainted dead away. In her mind's eye the truck tumbled down the hillside into the lake in one slow-motion movie moment.

Celia got up from her chair and walked to the door. "Where is that old devil anyway?" She opened the door and a cold breeze scented with wet scree and pine needles blew inside. Her mother always said *needles and pins* whenever a storm gathered. She'd worry her hands as she searched for candles and matches and firewood. It was the same when the preacher talked about God's great ending. Vanessa shivered, saying, *Needles and pins. Needles and pins*. Now Celia shivered. "Endings," she said, shaking her head.

She closed the door and turned to the cupboard to check out her candle and match supply. Plenty of white tapers and a few votives. It was possible the storm would blow itself out; the weather forecaster frequently called it wrong. Would there really be a winter storm coming in this early in the fall? Would the valley really be snowbound before Thanksgiving?

Ticking sounds scampered across the ceiling, down the wall, and across the floor. Celia clutched her chest and remembered to breathe.

When the preacher arrived in Etta's red car, it was four in the afternoon. He crossed the yard to the house, his stride like a bull's, turning his collar up against the winter chill. He rubbed the hem of his sweater trailing below his coat, knowing Celia wouldn't be happy with his decision. Even though he feared an emotional outburst, it had to be done. It was the only way he'd pay Vanessa's bill at the sanitarium. By the time he reached the porch, he was breathing hard. The driveway leading to the house was not that long. *Pathetic how out of shape I am*, he thought. He looked up and there she was, standing in the doorway.

"Whose car is that?" Celia stood aside as the preacher shoved his way into the steamy kitchen.

"Hmm, smells good in here," he said, looking around. He removed his jacket and hung it on a hook by the door.

"Where's your truck?"

"I already told you, it wouldn't start," he said. "A volunteer from the church loaned me hers until Tim can come out and jumpstart the old rattletrap."

"Generous volunteer," Celia said. "Are you ready for tea?"

The preacher nodded and took a seat at the picnic table. "That's how God wants to see us," he said. "Generous and obviously, always using impeccable scruples."

"If you're referring to me, God's looking in the wrong direction." She set the cup of steaming tea before her father. "But you know that, of course."

"Don't shortchange yourself," the preacher said. "Scruples are civilized. You've heard of them, I suppose?"

Celia glared. "Who cares," she said, refilling her wine glass with rosé. She carried it to the picnic table and sat across from her father.

Ed looked at his daughter with practiced compassion. "We'd be uncivilized without scruples, practically barbarians." He cleared his throat, raising his eyebrows as he took in her dull eyes, the shadows that had settled beneath each. It mattered little to his daughter, but he knew God cared about her despite her jezebel behavior. The preacher wanted her to love and be loved, to live a satisfying life. He knew that if he asked her she'd say she was satisfied, happy even. As if reading his thoughts, she narrowed her eyes over the edge of the wineglass. "What?"

He wanted to blush but resisted her challenge. She liked to embarrass him, to attack, wheedle the knife point into his underbelly; but really, her behavior was effective only in distancing them further from each other. He knew that God would call her out some day and she would have to drop to her knees and seek forgiveness.

Last year, when they stood around Star's pyre and he went crazy with the pain of losing a child, he embarrassed himself in front of his parishioners. Standing at the lake edge for the memorial service, the attendees were astounded by his violence. "Violence," he'd said in a sermon later, "is the Devil infiltrating the soul. I'm so sorry, forgive me please. In my weakened state, I turned away from God instead of toward Him."

The congregation seemed regretful, their judgment wounding the pastor in his most vulnerable state. He was taken back into the fold that day, learning a deeper lesson, he supposed. He took a sip of his tea and smiled at Celia.

It struck him as he set the mug down that he should forgive his daughter like he'd been forgiven. He reached a hand toward her. She didn't smile back, nor did she take his hand, just stared at the rosé she rolled around inside the smudged glass. Then she spoke, so quietly, the preacher had to lean closer to hear her.

"Remember those white flowers at the funeral, they were perfect for Star. My twin loved things that were pure, didn't she?"

"She did," the preacher agreed, and self-consciously drew his hand back from Celia and reached for the sugar bowl instead. He tried to catch her eyes as he stirred several teaspoons of the sweet crystals into his mug.

She looked up, challenging him again. "You said you had something important to tell me. What then?"

"Oh, that," he said, believing he was actually getting somewhere with his dark daughter. Perhaps it wasn't the right time to reveal his plan for bequeathing the little churchhouse to the sanitarium. "I…I was wondering, if you don't mind too much, I'd like to go through the sermons in the attic. At your convenience, of course."

"Star's stuff's up there," Celia said. "I'm not ready yet."

"I only need the boxes that contain your grandfather's and my sermons. I won't disturb anything else, if you don't mind."

"Not today, Daddy. Jay's coming."

"I wasn't expecting it to be today." He smiled and took a saltine with a square of cheese set neatly on top and slipped it into his mouth. Salt and sour spread across his tongue. He nodded. "Delicious."

Just past Firing Range Road, Jay waited at the clanging railroad crossing for the train to pass. The clacking wheels sparked, zinging light through the growing shadows. Electricity baffled him: zaps of current traveling through power lines, car batteries, house wiring, even the plug on the toaster that shorted one rainy morning when Celia plugged it in. He chuckled to himself, remembering her childish scream as sparks shot out from the socket and a small puff of smoke stunk up the kitchen. He rolled the window down and took a deep breath of the coming dusk.

The train thundered past, its whistle blasting. He fingered his gun belt, moving his hand slowly toward his holster. He'd brought his pistol along even though Captain said he wasn't allowed to carry it just yet. He turned to his open window. The horizon was black as a new bruise. He'd never admit it to anyone, but darkness frightened him. So open. So empty. His eagerness to see Celia grew with the weight and vibration of the barreling train. A breeze brushed his cheek and Jay could almost smell his girl's violet scent. His heartbeat quickened. Lightning flashed across the horizon, brightening the sky beyond the clanking cars. "Doll," he mouthed into the clamor of wheels and creaking cars. He undid his holster and drew his gun.

The barrel's cold metal touched his forehead. He could end his suffering this very moment. His finger clicked off the safety. He pressed the barrel harder to his forehead, denting his skin with the muzzle. *All it would take….* And just like that, he turned the gun to the open window and shot into the sky.

The sound was deafening. As his ears rang, Jay recalled his bullet striking his partner and Larry dropping to the ground. *I know he saw me raise my piece and aim at him,* Jay thought. No doubt Larry knew he was a dead man.

The last train car passed. The lights and bells stopped. The crossing gate rose. Everything was silent, except the hum of his rig, the distant rumble of the train, a peal of thunder, and the ringing in his ears. He holstered his gun. He shifted the cruiser into gear and carefully crossed the tracks.

The headlight beams lit his way. A foot of white stuff was expected overnight. It would shut down everything, including the electricity to the little churchhouse, all the way to Main Street and the hill community. Maybe even to the sanitarium. Some parts of town usually got off scot-free, all those patients, some needing life support; well it was a problem, power going out at a mental hospital. They had generators for backup, he supposed. You had to keep the patients warm, medicines chilled, food prepared, lights on.

Evening settled as Jay patrolled Firing Range Road. While the night set some people free, it made Jay feel naked. The last time he patrolled the Range beat, he'd switched off the headlights, hoping to go unnoticed. But when inkiness swallowed his car, panic gripped his chest. He had to pull over onto the gravel shoulder, open the window and gulp the night air.

In the distance he saw a red car turn out of Celia's driveway and head north toward town. She hadn't said anything about having a visitor prior to dinner. He furrowed his brow, speeding up a bit to see who was driving, but the car rounded the curve and he lost sight of it. Braking, he put on his blinker, readying the cruiser for the sharp turn into the long dirt driveway leading to the churchhouse.

Bumping into deep potholes, he shoved his distrust aside and pondered filling the holes with pea gravel. He'd bring in a yard or so, but not before it snowed, if the weather forecaster was correct, that is; he'd have to wait for spring before he'd get to fixing Celia's driveway. "Whatever!" he said, under his breath.

He shut off the cruiser and watched clouds building upon clouds, wild fringes of gray overlapping deep black and purple plumes, the setting sun lighting wispy edges. Storms invigorated him, while darkness weakened him. The engine clicked, cooling. Tiny ticks snapped the windshield, drops of rain as fine as the moisture on Celia's lashes after a shower.

He thought of her slim waist, her plump breasts, her.... He didn't want to lose her. Not for anything.

The last bit of sun leaked from between the clouds at the horizon. A strange glow lit the lake. Overhead stratus thickened—no sun filtered through from above. Jay shrugged. No one knew what lurked beneath Lake Monroe's still surface, nor for that matter, beneath his own calm demeanor. He imagined his therapist scratching his neatly trimmed beard as he pondered Jay's predicament. *The fag*, Jay thought and shifted in the cruiser seat. He felt the pinch of the ring box in his pocket. He shifted his weight again, tapping his hands on the steering wheel, readying himself for Doll's big surprise.

Mornings after the shooting, he would have stayed in bed if it hadn't been mandatory that he show up for a daily appointment with his designated therapist. The fag sat there waiting for him to talk about his feelings. Today was no different and while he played mum, picking at his cuticles, he pulled a tag of skin until a tiny pool of blood gathered in the trough edging the quick.

He rubbed a finger over the sore spot. He'd nailed Larry, that's what he'd done, all because he thought he'd seen the perp slipping through the shadows; in fact, he knew he'd seen him. *Goddammit!*

He'd shivered in the therapist's office. Who knew why, but the therapist jumped on him at that exact moment: "What? What were you thinking just now?" he'd said.

"Nothing," Jay said, but that wasn't true. He'd been thinking about Doll, imagining his dick sliding between her adept fingers. "God," he groaned into the cruiser's silent interior; he got hard right there in the therapist's office. Squeezing his thighs together didn't help; neither did trying not to look at the picture of the blonde bombshell the therapist kept on his desk: golden bouffant hair circling her glowing face like a halo. The sun poured through a single small window that faced the street. He imagined pulling some reckless driver out of his car and roughing him up. The image cooled Jay down a bit.

He turned to the little churchhouse now and saw Celia waving through the window. He waved back, lust baiting him again. He was completely in love with her, something he'd told Larry that night while they sat together in the dark interior of the car, waiting for the perp. The dark had weakened him that night too, and the subject of love, Larry for his wife and children, and Jay for Ceal—a gal that some found inappropriate mating material for a cop—but it was his own damn business, wasn't it? He couldn't be thrown off the force for dating a girl who made her living twirling around a stripper pole, could he? He fingered the ring box in his pocket as he climbed from the car, grinning.

In the west, weighty clouds crumpled like a rear-end accident. Both Larry and Star had had bad luck; some folks just did. The live ones were the lucky ones, or so it seemed. The churchhouse door opened and Celia shouted, "JJ!"

He turned, watching her leap down the stairs, bounding like a deer across the lawn toward him. *Lively*, he thought as he caught her in his arms and swung her around, nuzzling his face into her black curls, smelling her scent of violets. Her eyes were so dark they practically buckled his knees. "Sweetie," he said, and kissed her long and hard, lifting her off the ground, his arms wrapped so tightly around her waist that he thought his love for her might crush her. "You see the sky?" he said.

She turned her face upward, squinting impishly.

He could see the breath leaving her lips, a frail wisp in the biting air. The curve of her cheekbone. The pucker below her full lips. *Good God! She was a beauty.*

"Storm's coming," she said, watching the sky for a few moments before turning back to him, her face filled with excitement. "Dan says we're not closing shop, even if we do get a foot of snow." She shrugged from his arms. "So, what's my surprise?"

"I know how you love the boat shed. I'll show you up top." He grabbed her hand.

"JJ," she said, pulling back. "Show me inside. It's cold out here."

He scooped an arm around her and hustled her along, his panic temporarily abated with his girl at his side.

She pulled back and stared at him, a quizzical look knitting her dark brows.

He stepped back as well. "What's wrong, Babe?"

"Come on," she said, jamming her fists onto her waist. "You're acting funny. Give it up. What's my surprise?"

"Hey," he said, his voice smooth. He knew how to calm people with the tone of his voice: low, steady, even. He laughed a little. *Nervous*, he thought. "I could say the same. What's bothering you?"

She rubbed her head and looked at the ground, her fingers kneading her crown.

"Someone bugging you, that red car leaving the driveway?" he said, raising his eyebrows. "Someone from the club giving you trouble, or something?"

"That was Daddy," she laughed, dropping her hand, shaking her black curls incredulously. "I already said everything's okay. So, did you meet with that new guy, Johnny what's-his-name?"

"Johnny America. He's a jock, at least that's what the gal in files says. She's got all the girl's gossiping about Officer America. Maybe then they'll forget…."

"That would be good, you'd be off the hook, not that you were ever…."

Celia looped her arm through Jay's. "Well, never mind. The sky," she said, "it's a weird color, don't you think?"

"Freak storm's coming, like the one that rolled through last spring." He sniffed the air. "Smells like chicken and snow."

He unhooked her arm and took her hand, leading her up the rickety stairs. The deck above the boat shed, with its familiar smell of musty life vests and rotting rubber flippers, was in dire need of repair. From the catwalk, the blackened patch of scorched earth where the preacher had burnt Star's pyre wasn't only an eyesore, but an ongoing reminder of the family's loss. Why it hadn't grown over was beyond him. Beyond the scorched patch, reeds and giant lilies, brown edged and curling, bobbed in the ruffling water. He leaned over the rail and tried to see the boat they'd pulled under the overhang two summers ago. He could just make out the peeling bow.

On the far side of the lake, a murder of cawing crows lifted off bare branches and settled again. Beyond that, he could see the thick wall of rain heading toward them. "Sheez, we're gonna get it," he said, sucking in his breath as he reached a hand inside his coat pocket, feeling the ring box.

Celia grabbed his sleeve and pulled, turning his hand over to see what he was holding. "Gum? I thought," she said, her mouth turning down.

He folded a stick of peppermint into his mouth. Lifting a finger to her forehead to push a wisp of hair out of her face, he said, "No pouting, Doll." He shook his head. "God, you're killing me with those lips."

"You're killing me," she said, and shoved her left hand in front of his face, waggling her ring finger. "See anything interesting here?"

There they were, long slender fingers edged with silky lacquer. No jewelry, nothing to make her more beautiful, and if anyone asked, Jay would have to say bare is best, all he needed was his girl, no makeup, no clothes, nadda. He took her hand and kissed each finger. "Beautiful," he said, just as the rain started, a wall of fat drops splashing straight down. "Look," he said, pointing.

Celia turned, her face rosy from the cold. "A rainbow," she squealed.

While she was looking away, Jay reached back into his jacket pocket and brought out the ring box.

The smell of mothballs mixed with the smell of cacciatore and wafted around Celia as she pulled down a quilt from the top shelf, aware as always that Star's ashes sat in a metal urn in the back corner of the bedroom closet. She turned off the closet light and stood for a moment facing the darkened window. The wind blew steadily now and what few leaves left on the apple trees broke free, streaking past the rattling glass. For a moment, Celia imagined Star's ashes drifting skywards as she emptied them from the urn beneath an apple tree in the orchard beyond the churchhouse.

As she floated the blanket over the bed, the engagement ring caught the overhead light, flashing like moonlight sparkling across the lake. It was a delicate band with a tiny diamond resting on three silver prongs. *Very nice choice, JJ,* she thought, turning to the bathroom door, listening to the water running, imagining him standing before the sink in his skivvies, checking his physique in the mirror. He was a handsome man: square chin, gray eyes, and hair cut short in the police academy style. It gave him a look of power—or possibly menace—which she didn't mind since she knew he was a real pussycat. Still, his emotional intensity sometimes frightened her.

She felt ambivalent about wedlock. It was the word *lock* she supposed, that tightened her insides. And then there was the *subject* they didn't like talking about—Star and Larry's deaths and the pain they both still suffered. They each expected the other to get over the grief, but Jay's wound was fresher—still festering. A bullet through a buddy's neck was difficult for a soft-hearted person to move past. Any person, she imagined, would have trouble getting over such a horrible accident.

Celia shivered, feeling the red silk of her blouse cool against her shoulders, clinging still from running back to the house through the rain. Dinner was mostly delicious, though somewhat burnt. Jay didn't seem to mind, eating two platefuls with gusto. She smiled as she recalled him relishing his food.

As she unbuttoned her blouse, the bathroom door opened and he stepped into the bedroom. He dropped onto the side of the bed facing her, leaning close to lift her hand with the engagement ring, stroking each finger gently. Tingles dissolved her—that was the thing about him; he had her number. She leaned in to kiss him just as the floorboards overhead creaked. They both looked up at the ceiling, then back to each other in wonder.

"Barometric pressure," he said. "Storm's coming in."

She nodded, though she wasn't sure she believed it was the wind moaning the old house. If it were Star's ghost, she was pushing the heavy overstuffed chair they'd hauled home from the junk store across the attic floor. Star's way of letting Celia know that having a man in their parents' old bed gave her the willies.

Now Jay and she were about to climb under the covers of the very bed Daddy had promised wasn't worth loading into the truck and hauling to the dump. Another creak from above and Celia shook her head. "I've been hearing spooky sounds lately." She finished unbuttoning her blouse and dropped it to the floor. "You know…strange clicking noises. I've looked all over the place but can't seem to figure out where they're coming from. Or what is making them."

"Could just be a loose shingle or the phone line dangling from the eave. I'll take a look for you in the morning."

"It's not outside. The sounds are coming from the walls and the ceiling. Even at work I hear them. It's like they follow me everywhere I go." She slid her hand over JJ's thigh, slipping her fingers beneath the waistband of his skivvies.

He leaned in, pressing his warm lips to hers. "Mice?" he breathed, pushing bra straps off her shoulders and kissing each breast.

"Alabaster's a good mouser. But I guess…."

Jay kissed her bare neck. "Why don't you call in sick tonight," he whispered. "You can tell your boss later that you'll be quitting."

Celia pulled away. "But I'm not quitting." She studied Jay's face. His expression flattened, jaw tightening the muscles of his cheeks.

"You're engaged to a public servant now, Ceal," he said, raising one eyebrow. He lay back on the bed and pulled Celia inside the bend of his arm, stroking her hair gently. "You need to dress respectably. You know, be a good representative of the Force."

"You sound just like Daddy," she said. "An engagement doesn't mean you own me. In fact, I haven't said *yes* yet." She tried to sit up, but he held her firmly.

"Shhh," he said, sliding his hand over her ribs and into the curve of her waist.

She sighed and turned her attention to the sound of hail, tiny snow pellets dashing themselves against the windowpanes. She smelled his soapy scent and his nutty gun-oil odor that had become so much a part of him she no longer thought of it as special, just Jay.

"You're with me now," Jay said, and rolled on top of her.

The night sky seemed to glow; a marvel Jay hadn't seen since he was a boy. As he stood on the front porch, his nakedness now a relief in the darkness, Celia stepped outside and stood next to him. He turned to her, taking in her earthy scent, wrapping an arm around her petite shoulders. "Noctilucent clouds," he pointed westward. "See, no moonlight, yet the clouds glow."

"Looks like heaven," she said, and ran a warm hand down his back. "We slept a long time, didn't we?"

"Slept?" He kissed her head. "You slept! I was ready to go again."

"Oh," she said, leaning close. "You should have awakened me."

"Later," he said, thinking Celia seemed tipsy, the way she slid her hand inside his, the way her weight fell against his shoulder. "You okay?"

"It's cold out here. And there's hail on the ground." She squeezed closer, sighing. "Hold me, JJ."

He pulled her against him. "If the clouds part, we might see a shooting star." The word *shoot* caused his throat to tighten. He cleared it, trying not to think of Larry lying on the ground next to the sheet metal shed. He remembered Celia's sister, Star, so beautiful and bright, like a willow tree dusted with moonlight. He imagined Celia was thinking about her as well, for as she rested her head on his shoulder, her face dampened against his bare arm. He was reaching a hand to wipe the tears from her cheeks when she lifted her head, stiffening.

"There, by the shore," she pointed.

"What?"

"It's Star. See? By the willow tree."

"Doll," he drew her shivering body closer, "it's just the night shining clouds reflecting off the hail."

She pushed him away. "It's Star. She's trying to reach me. I already told you that."

"Let her go, Sweetie," Jay said. "Please, just let her go."

Celia threw off his arm and bolted inside. The door banged loudly, echoing off the lake.

Jay followed her in, standing quietly behind her. She kneeled by the woodstove, speaking to Alabaster softly as she stoked the fire. For some reason her petite back made him remember the breakfasts his frail mother had fixed him when he was a child, pancakes with melted butter and pools of Aunt Jemima spilling over the stack. Once back from dog shift, he'd make Celia coffee and pancakes, bring her a tray of food in bed. And afterwards, he'd take a plate to Larry's house. The last time he'd stopped, Larry's kids had just finished soupy bowls of Rice Krispies and were settled at their kitchen table with Mickey Mouse coloring books. He'd see what, if anything, Larry's widow needed before the storm locked the valley down.

Fire flamed up hot. Celia rose from where she crouched by the stove and left the room. Jay lingered for a few minutes listening to the wood snap and pop then headed into the bedroom. Celia stood by the window, rolling her thumb over the engagement ring, turning it round and round her finger.

"You like it, Doll?"

"Like what?" she said, her back remaining to him.

"You know." He stepped behind her, wrapping his arms around her waist. "The ring."

She turned inside his arms, chewing her plump bottom lip. "It's beautiful, JJ. But you know I'm not quitting my job—it's how I make my living. So, I guess that puts it back in your court." She untangled herself from his arms and climbed into bed.

Celia curled into a fetal position, listening to the dishes clink and silverware jangle as Jay cleaned up the mess she'd made. When he finally came to bed, she feigned sleep. She wanted to wrap her arms around him, get him to forgive her for not being more grateful for the beautiful diamond, but a hard place had taken hold in her chest and it wasn't budging. She stayed still until she heard his breathing slide, then turned onto her side to face him. She did love him. Why did she always have to spoil everything? She reached out a hand and rested it on his chest while listening for the house to groan.

Finally, after dozing a bit, she roused herself to dress for work. He'd asked her to quit her job—which was as ridiculous as wanting her to wear dowdy clothing. What was wrong with everyone, couldn't they just accept her for who she was?

Celia slipped out of bed and walked soundlessly into the bathroom. She flipped on the light and studied her sad reflection in the mirror. It was hard to look herself in the eye. It wasn't that she was ashamed of her reflection; it was that she felt so deeply bruised right now that it made her sick to witness her own bone pain. She leaned close to the mirror, imagining she might see a path leading out of the emotional uncertainty she constantly wrestled with, but she saw only flatness that reminded her of a gray overcast sky.

She looked away, turned on the water and splashed her face. As she dried her pale skin, the clicking started again. It came from the bedroom this time, louder than she'd heard it before. A leap of fright jumped in her chest. Holding her breath, she crept into the bedroom, hoping to catch Star manifesting from the afterlife, standing by the window.

Her cat leapt down from the dresser and wove between her ankles, purring loudly. She bent down and stroked his back, whispering, "That was you?" Relieved, she left the cat and walked around to JJ's side of the bed. She returned the ring to the tiny box and set it on the nightstand. Jay's chest rose and fell steadily beneath the quilted blankets, his fingers curling easily into his palms, his eyes darting beneath relaxed lids as he slept.

"The answer is no, Baby." She tucked the blanket up under his chin. "See you in the morning." Silently, she turned and left the room.

CHAPTER FOUR

Celia buttoned her winter coat at the neck and pulled the hood up over her head. She switched on the porch light and stepped into the icy black night. The smell of sleet and applewood smoke made her linger a moment, breathing deeply the spicy wetness, feeling like everything was going to be all right, even though she'd turned down Jay's marriage proposal. Just knowing that he loved her was all that mattered.

The moon broke through the clouds causing the lake and sleet-covered ground to glow. For the moment, Celia resigned herself to forgetting her twin. She crunched down the icy steps, feeling buoyant as she maneuvered across the slippery yard to the trail rounding the north end of the lake.

"Dancing tonight will do me good," she said, and began to think about the new moves she and Raven choreographed: back bends, snaky arms, sultry hands, shimmies, and splits.

She hurried along the icy path, her mind turning to the black net stockings she'd purchased at the shoe store earlier that week and the swishing sound they'd make as she sauntered across the stage. She knew they'd inspire her customers, giving them the fever. Even with the cold burning her cheeks, a fine mist of sweat dampened her upper lip at the imagined dance she would do for the audience. Then she thought of Donna returning Celia's missing fuchsia bra, and her lie that she'd found it tossed beneath a table in the lounge. Confused, Celia thought one of the barmaids could have swiped it, but when Donna was dressing and bent to buckle her shoes, Celia saw past the dancer to the picture she'd taped inside her locker. She saw a photo of Celia wearing the sequined bra with a cutout of Donna's face taped over hers. Celia turned red-hot. She wanted to shove the dancer inside the locker and shout,

"I'm the star here, not you, understand?" Instead, she swallowed her rage and snatched the bra out of Donna's hands. Back at the makeup mirror she could see a reflection of Donna taking down the photo and slipping it beneath a stack of folded clothing in the bottom of her locker. When she turned to see if Celia was looking, Celia glared at her. Donna shrank from the room.

"She's trying to steal my spotlight," Celia said, surprised by the fierceness of her words startling the silence of the night. She remembered Jay standing on the porch after they'd made love. Only the hardy could stand outside in the cold in just the birthday suit. Jay was hot-blooded and it would take a good half-hour under the night sky to cool him down. He said the cold enhanced his sleeping phase; helped him get past the *vulture thoughts*, thoughts that preyed on him when everything dissolved into the quiet of the night.

Celia imagined slipping the palm of her hand over his smooth shoulders, drawing it down his back to the warm dip above his buttocks. A shudder rolled through her. Wednesday nights always had Dan in a "frying-pan-mood"—Raven's words for the day their boss paid bills. She could have stayed snug in bed with her lover, but with Jay harping about her clothing choices and how she'd have to behave like a *good cop's wife* once married, she needed the escape of dance. She glanced up at the *lunatic* clouds, or whatever he called them, and her eyes filled with tears. She pressed on, Star's old boots steadying her as she headed along the dark path into the woods.

She knew the trail's ups and downs like she knew the nuances of arousal; it was a game she often played, seeing how long she could walk into the ever-darkening forest without switching on the penlight she carried in her coat pocket. Tonight, the forest was brighter than usual, the sleet having dressed every limb, needle, and leftover fall leaf in white. Jay's clouds seemed to brighten everything as well.

Celia heard a night hawk and figured she'd made it about halfway through the forest without turning on her penlight. A twig snapped off to her right. The hair on the back of her neck rose. She stopped, standing statue-still, listening hard. Another snap and then her fingers moved nervously inside her pocket, locating the switch on her light. She was about to flick it on when before her, a wavering luminosity cast faint twisted tree shadows across the path. She looked around. Where were the familiar landmarks, the odd bend of the pine limb, the basalt outcrop, the…?

Her heart thrummed in her ears. A dog barked somewhere beyond the woods. Clumps of sleet dropped from the trees, flopping to the ground. All at once, Celia was devoured by a sweet scent. "Violets," she whispered, recalling the last time she'd smelled the tiny blossoms it was spring and she was standing between her parents before her twin's headstone. The smell was so strong that she'd looked around for a patch of purple flowers, half-expecting to find a large clump of violets growing nearby. But not one flower could be seen.

The scent grew more potent and the light brightened. Celia stepped back, feeling the sturdiness of a tree trunk behind her. She pressed against it, letting it support her back as she slid to a crouch. "Who's there?"

The light expanded, willing the woods to daylight. Enveloped by the sugary scent, Celia felt lightheaded, altered, almost drifting outside herself. She whispered, "What's happening?"

"It's just me, silly girl!" Star's words formed inside Celia's head as clearly as if her twin stood beside her. "Look at you all crouched down like a scared dog. You're not afraid of me, are you?"

"Star?" Celia said, feeling the wetness of tears on her cheeks. She wiped them away with the back of her hand, watching her sister's shimmering light-dress billow around her like a silk scarf on a breezy day. "I knew you'd come back." Celia's voice sounded oddly inhuman in the drippy woods. "I told Raven so." She brought her hand to her throat, feeling the vibration of her words as she spoke. "Even the cards promised your return from the dead."

The light pulsed, illuminating the pine forest like day. "There's no such thing as dead," Star said, light sparking and popping around her. "I'm here, see? I'm with you, sweet sister. I always am."

Celia opened her mouth to speak, but no words came out.

"Silly Sissy," Star said, blonde locks floating around her head, great golden tendrils streaming like in her dream: the two of them tangled together beneath the surface of Lake Monroe. "Don't worry. It wasn't your fault, just my time to go, that's all."

Celia cried, "Daddy doesn't believe me. He blames me for your death."

"He'll change his mind," Star said. "Now I have something I need you to do for me."

Shivering, Celia drew the hood more tightly around her face. "Anything!"

"You must," Star said, "make Daddy confess his sin."

"I told him," Celia said, "when you fell overboard, you were trying to convince me of something. What was it, Star? I can't remember."

The light pulsed more rapidly. "You were so young, sweet sister," Star said, reaching out a vaporous hand to touch Celia. "We were little children. You must demand the truth."

Celia reached toward the light, her fingers meeting Star's. A chill washed through her and she drew back. The violet scent in the woods thickened.

"Ask him about his visits to the attic," Star said, and her light flashed, causing Celia to shield her eyes. "I saw everything."

The light began to fade along with the smell of violets, leaving Celia alone in the dripping woods. "Sissy?" Celia said. "Don't go. Please, don't leave me alone."

The woods dropped into darkness. Celia stayed crouched against the tree, weeping softly, the drips and creaks loud around her. At last, she shook herself from her malaise, pulled herself together and stood, steadying herself against the trunk of the tree. She remembered the penlight and flicked it on, shining it around the woods, looking for the remains of her sister's visitation. The rocks and bent trunks were strangers to her; her disorientation was complete.

Shaking, she turned and bolted through the darkness, back toward the little churchhouse and the familiar comfort of Jay's arms.

Star's words echoed through her head as she raced along the woodland path, grabbing for limbs, stumbling over rocks, tripping on roots, catching herself and running on, coat flapping, breath coming in burning gulps. *Make Daddy confess his sin,* Star had said. Sissy's words made Celia feel raw. Her stomach gripped; her terror propelled her onward.

"Jay," she screamed, ducking where she knew a gnarled branch reached across the path. But the night was black and she ducked too late. The limb snapped her in the face. Jerking sideways, she went down on her hands and knees onto a pile of sharp basalt. Pain shot through her. An owl screeched. Her heart lurched. Scrambling to her feet, she ran on, hysterical now. At last the black surface of the lake came into view and she stopped long enough to catch her breath, looking back to see if the misty veil had followed. She saw nothing but inky darkness.

Star's streaming light had been close enough for Celia to touch. But was it really Sissy? Celia shook to the core. Taking off again, her boots crunched on the slippery sleet, arms flailing the icy air as she slip-ran toward the warm glow of the churchhouse.

CHAPTER FIVE

Jay clung to his story against all reason, the idea that he could have prevented the shooting. As he walked into the too-warm kitchen, he decided Celia might feel equally responsible for Star's death. If so, she had to be feeling guilty as hell, just as he was.

She'd left the ring box next to the bed. Did that mean *no*? He could see it would be hard for her to say *yes*. After all, she was still getting over the loss of her sister. But did she have to be so secretive? And running off to work like that on the night he proposed? He shook his head. They could still be entwined beneath the warm bed covers.

He grabbed open the refrigerator door and leaned in. The cool air smelling of cacciatore, soothed him—like the touch of Celia's chilly hand to the small of his back. He thought back to their lovemaking and shuddered involuntarily. She was amazing in bed.

He grabbed the bottle of milk from the fridge and poured a tall glass, lifting it to his lips just as heavy boots clunked up the stairs. The door banged open. He whirled to see Celia's tear-streaked face, her torn jeans, blood staining her knees and palms.

"No, no…," Jay shouted, spilling the milk as he banged the glass down on the counter. He sprinted across the kitchen, steadying her in his strong grip. "What happened?"

"She's out there." Celia held out her bloody hands as she collapsed into his arms.

"Who's out there? Who did this to you?" Jay helped her to the kitchen sink. "I told you not to walk through the woods. Goddammit, Ceal." He took both her hands and held them beneath warm running water.

"Shit, be careful," she said. "It stings!"

"Hold still," Jay said, shifting his stance as Celia's weight dropped against him.

Celia gulped between sobs, "I got lost in the woods and then I tripped and fell in the scree. I landed on all fours. It was horrible."

He gently dried her hands with a towel. "It's deep. You'll need stitches," he said and pressed napkins over the injuries. "Press your palms together. It'll stop the bleeding."

"My knees…."

Jay helped her to the rocker. "That's why I don't want you walking through the woods to work. See, you were followed. It's dangerous out there. You're lucky…."

"I know, I know," she said.

Jay helped her out of the torn and bloody jeans. "Your knees," he said, "they'll need stitches too." He headed for the bathroom, returning with a bag of cotton balls and Bactine. He cleaned her knees and sprayed them with ointment. "You're out of Band-Aids," he said, and covered the injuries with napkins. "We'll pick up some at the hospital pharmacy once we get there." He looked at his watch; it wasn't long until he was to meet up with his new partner, Johnny. He'd radio him once he got Celia settled in the cruiser.

"You've got work, JJ," she said. "Just go. I'll be fine."

"I'm taking you to the hospital. But first, I'll check outside for the perp." Jay slipped on his boots and coat and grabbed the fire poker from beside the woodstove. He leaned in and kissed Celia's forehead. "I have my keys. Don't unlock the door for anyone. Hear me?"

She nodded.

A half-hour later, Celia heard Jay's boots on the steps, the key turning in the lock. He burst into the kitchen, the fire poker gripped in his right hand, looking cop-like. "Nada. I walked around the north end of the lake. It's dark, you know. I couldn't see much. Probably some perv from the club's stalking you." Jay crossed the floor to the telephone. He set the poker on the counter and picked up the receiver to dial the precinct.

"Please, don't call it in." Celia wiped her eyes with the back of her hand. "It was probably a practical joke. No one got hurt."

"You've got gashes in your knees and palms. If that isn't hurt, I don't know what is. And if there's someone hiding out there, scaring my woman, the Force needs to know about it." He dropped the receiver in the cradle and moved to the refrigerator.

"We'll ice your knees while I get ready for work." He took out an ice tray and wrapped cubes in a towel. "I'm worried about you. The perp could turn violent next time." Jay sat down next to her and peeled back the throw. "I'm driving you to work from now on."

"Right! How would that look, a stripper arriving in a cop car?" Celia said, wishing he wouldn't fuss so much. "Dan's going to give me hell for having banged up my *gorgeous legs*." She started to cry again. "He'll give my spot to Donna."

"That's the least of your worries," he said, and peeled off the bloody napkins. "What the hell?" He dropped the icepack on the floor. Cubes scattered across the floor in all directions. Jay jumped to his feet and began pacing back and forth. He crossed his arms over his chest and stopped to face Celia. "What's going on here?"

She shrugged. "How should I know?"

Perfect pink flesh rounded Celia's knees. She removed the towel from her hands and turned her palms upright in her lap. They were flawless as well, smooth and rosy beneath the bare kitchen bulb. Gasping, she drew fingers up over her thighs. The burn scars were gone as well.

"It's the miracle, JJ. You know, like the Monroes have. Well, the men in the family have had, that is. And now me."

"You're joking, right?"

Celia shook her head. She felt like crying and laughing at the same time. "Jay, it's the Monroe Miracle. You know, Daddy's toe and Grandpa's drowning. I'm not shitting you—I've received the miracle!"

Jay looked at his watch. "I gotta meet Johnny down at Peggo's Grill, pronto."

"JJ, you got to believe me. Please?" Celia grabbed his arm. "You washed out my cuts. You said they were deep. You thought I needed stitches."

Jay shook himself free from Celia's grip and crossed the room. He removed his gun belt from the door hook and buckled it around his waist. He grabbed his coat and opened the door. The sound of sleet on the lake peppered the silence. "I don't know what to believe, Celia," he said, shaking his head. He brought a hand to his forehead and stood there for a few moments, cold streaming in around him. "Stay home and keep the door locked, okay?" He slammed the door closed and disappeared into the night.

CHAPTER SIX

Celia pushed aside her robe and touched the perfect skin gracing her bare thighs. Each time she ran her fingers over the smooth texture, a bit of her bone pain wisped away like a curl of applewood smoke rising from the chimney. She wanted to tell JJ that her sister was back, but when he saw the miraculous healing, he looked beyond her, eyes wide, mouth open, as if bloody words had been scrawled across the kitchen walls by some evil poltergeist.

Celia had called after him, "Jay! JJ wait, come back!" But quickly his boots on the stairs and crunch of tires in the driveway were replaced by the sound of hail peppering the roof.

The churchhouse was quiet, with the exception of the creak of the rocking chair and the pop of the woodstove. Celia continued to hope that he would return. She ran her fingertips back and forth across her healed palms and listened for his cruiser. Finally, she gave up on JJ and wandered off to bed. Snug beneath the covers, Alabaster curled against her back. Celia slept like the dead.

The sun reflected brightly off the hail, awakening her early; the daylight was nearly as intense as her sister's light. She felt compelled to tell someone about Star's visitation and decided only her mother would understand. She'd tell her the next time she visited Luna Sanitarium.

She got out of bed and pulled on her robe, wandering into the kitchen. The fire was soon burning hot and she was sitting at the kitchen table with a cup of coffee, expecting JJ's squad car to roll through the brightness any minute.

As she sipped the steaming brew, her thoughts turned to Vanessa's upright figure sitting unresponsive in a wheelchair. She'd say, "I've been blessed, Mama, with the Monroe Miracle."

No one, not even Daddy, can deny it, she thought. Whether Mama understood her or not was unclear. They say folks in comas hear everything; however, Vanessa, the doctor said, was only in a state of shock, not a coma. It was like she was frozen in time. She was a statue of sorts.

The fire snapped, the eaves dripped, a rabbit darted from the hail-weighted weeds across the wide expanse of yard. Celia frowned; could the burn scars come back? If she didn't behave herself, would she be punished like Daddy said she would?

Mewing, Alabaster jumped onto the picnic bench beside her. Celia drew a hand through his soft fur. No Monroe woman had ever had a healing, which could only mean that it was only the men who deserved such splendor. She wondered if her daddy, who'd nearly sliced off his little toe, had felt the euphoria she felt. The way he'd told the story, the memory was more a rolling-around-on-the-ground-in-excruciating-pain sort of incident, rather than an experience of pleading with God for relief. So, when the pain did disappear, he knew at once that the miracle had touched him and that God expected him to carry on what the others had preached before him: the truth of the risen Lord. He was just eighteen when he walked into Bible College, all ten toes intact.

A spray of hail drifted off bare apple branches beyond the lake, glistening in the sunshine as it swept toward the ground. Celia thought about how the Toi Toy Club had once stored hundreds of bins of apples within its chilled walls. Her grandfather told the story of climbing the fruit ladder to pick a bumper crop of Winesaps. Most were carted away, he'd said, washed and stored to sell throughout the winter and spring; many were sold at market, the rest ended up in the churchhouse's root cellar, either overflowing in bushel baskets or gleaming in jars as sauce.

Her grandfather had repeated his story of the Monroe Miracle every Thanksgiving while they boiled his traditional penuche candy to soft-ball stage. He told the twins that the rung on his old orchard ladder broke unexpectedly and how his fall to the ground far below happened in slow motion. It was always the same, Grandfather's description of a broken tibia—sweat soaking his clothing, his screams frightening off crows that'd settled to peck at the unpicked fruit dangling above him.

"I writhed like a snake clean through the clear of night," he exclaimed. But then, like the preacher, Celia's grandfather's pain vanished. By morning, he got to his feet, tested the leg, and then miraculously climbed the ladder, avoiding the broken rung, thanking God with each step as he climbed higher. He ate several apples then finished picking the bumper crop. The next day he headed for town to enroll in Bible College. By the end of the story the penuche had cooled enough for Star and Celia to enjoy its brown-sugary goodness.

Celia adjusted the robe over her bare legs and recalled that the preacher had wanted to talk to her about something important, but as her father sipped tea, he spoke only of his plans to go through the old sermons stored in the attic—at her convenience, of course. She half-expected him to make another case for why God wanted her to give up exotic dancing. She would like to explain to the preacher that like her great-grandfather's baptismal drowning and resurrection, she also had experienced the Monroe Miracle. She recalled her daddy reciting the story to his weeping congregation, the violet-scented grass, Celia's great-grandfather suddenly spouting water, sitting up and exclaiming: *Praise the Lord*. His eyes were wide, his *being* drenched in cold lake water, and he was vitally alive.

Alabaster butted his head against Celia's forearm. "Sweet kitty," she cooed. "Yes, Mama's the one to tell. And you, of course." She scratched the cat behind the ears; purring, he lifted his paw to Celia's arm. The weight of his paw brought back her worry. How could she get JJ to understand that the miracle healing didn't mean she was a witch? He'd made it clear how much he disliked her visits from Raven—*That card reading witch. I don't trust her*.

Celia squirmed, recalling waking early, enveloped in sweat. She'd dreamed that the glowing end of a burning stick had branded her upper thigh. She turned and buried her face in JJ's pillow, smelling his scent. She looked up, seeing the ring box on the nightstand. Reaching for the box, she removed the delicate band and slipped it back onto her finger. She didn't *need* to turn down his offer of marriage—he would take back the ring the first chance he got anyway.

CHAPTER SEVEN

During the summer months Raven tacked winter quilts over the bedroom windows and wet them down like her family did in the south. Then, even during very humid conditions, a quilt and a fan rendered the room swamp-cool so she would sleep well at night. Now the quilts were piled high on her bed, as winter chilled her tiny place like a cool box of ice.

She climbed out of bed and dressed in her favorite lavender sweat suit, which she noticed still smelled like the bacon grease she'd rubbed down the woodstove with yesterday. She'd polished its surface with a rag until the stovetop gleamed deep black. She knew her Mama, if she'd been there, would approve of the shine. Then she put on the kettle and made herself a cup of chicory tea. It was a morning ritual to sit by the window and muse over an upturned card—not that she believed in reading cards, but she did believe in the family tradition. All the women in her clan were card readers.

She sipped her tea then shuffled the deck. The card she picked was the Ace of Spades. Hair on the back of Raven's neck prickled. A mini vision flitted across her mind: Cece falling. "Sugar," she whispered, tapping the card with her fingernail. If her grandmother were here, she would know exactly what it meant, but Raven wasn't tetched like the other women in the family—well, perhaps a little. But decidedly, little Sugar could be in danger, and when the time was right, Raven would warn her.

She folded the cards together, placing the frayed stack inside the worn velvet bag and returned it to the drawer by the sink. Carefully she washed her teacup. She dried everything, including the splatters on the counter and the sink edge. She rubbed lotion into her dry hands and looked around the tiny place, feeling satisfied. She turned out the lights and locked the door.

Outside, the hail had begun to melt in the blazing sun, the smell of it reminding her of lake mud and nutmeg. Raven stretched her quads, then her Achilles, considering which trail she'd take past the firing range to Cece's house. She spoke aloud into the chill of morning, "North, since the ragweed's wet down good now."

She took off running down the path toward the firing range, jogging past clumps of grass bent over by the hail. Each step jarred her hip; she jabbed a thumb into her left gluteal until the pain eased up a bit. *Thud-thud-thud.*

Running along, her mind tuned to William, imagining his long fingers stroking her bare breasts. "Beautiful naked man," she breathed. "We should go bowlin' or better still—ballin'."

She rounded the corner and there in the distance a glint of blue sweet water. She missed the river, but Lake Monroe eased her yearning. "Movin' along," she said, and then for some reason thought of the sale coming up at the thrift store, Easy Come, Easy Go. She'd meet Cece there, pick out costumes for the new dance number that had been whirling around inside her head. They would have a blast.

Whoooomp! Dirt from a mortar shell flew into the air not fifty yards beyond the barbwire fence up ahead. Raven stumbled backwards, nearly slipping in a shady place where the hail remained frozen. "Don't you fuckin' know," she shouted, swinging her arm at the field. "The fuckin' war is over." She whirled around, catching herself before she fell, kicking a big clump of hail from atop a mass of tangled grass. "Fuck 'em. Fuck 'em all."

Raven imagined Donna's mouth uttering those very words; she hated Donna taking sides, complaining about Cece. "A horrible dancer, and too fat," is exactly what she'd said. Raven wasn't the going-along-with-others type, more like the get-even type. She'd seen the picture of Cece taped inside Donna's locker and the missing fuchsia brassiere tangled in with a mess of costumes. Raven turned around that day and walked the other way—deciding on a plan—something that would get Donna real good. But then Cece discovered Donna's sick ways on her own—and that was that.

She shook the adrenalin rush out of her big hands and took off again, running past the remnants of the Monroe's oldest orchard, the vantage point where she'd first seen the little churchhouse from a distance, a spiral of smoke lifting from its chimney, sliding over the eaves, drifting down through the gnarled orchard.

She stopped there, studying the landscape, the sky, and smelling the air. The hailstorm was only a warning—a blizzard was on its way. *Sky says it's comin'*, Raven thought, *that's for sure. Things turn quick around here—like friendship does. A meal together—baby back ribs and sauce, corn pone and rye whiskey. Uh-huh, that would be grand. She'd invite William, beautiful William.*

She wondered if her mama would approve of William. She recalled the bus approaching and her mama standing close at her side, pulling her collar around her pin-curled head. Raven smiled. That big winter coat just about drowned the little woman. Raven wanted to give her a quick kiss and say, "Don't cry, Mama. Army life will be good for me, you know, structure's somethin' I need." And then she couldn't say more because the knot in her throat had turned too hard. Raven climbed onboard the bus and sat with her leather suitcase between her feet. She watched out the window at her mama waving goodbye, growing tinier by the moment. It was for the best, with Daddy long run off now and her siblings all worthless. At least this way she could send a check home each month.

She came around the corner to the trailhead leading to Lake Monroe. In the bowl of land next to the lake lolled Cece's little churchhouse, all hail-capped and sparkling in the sun. A curl of smoke rose from the chimney.

Celia sat up, her attention vigilant as she'd seen something along the lake trail, a flash of movement. "Star?" Looking hard through the frost-edged glass, she searched the reeds for her sister, all the while her heart pounded with excitement. Another flash of movement and Celia jumped up from the picnic table, calling out "Star" as she ran to the door. She flung it open. A clump of hail fell from the trees beyond the lake, moisture drifting in a shimmering spray. She watched the cloud drift off, then examined the trail again for movement. Raven rounded the corner of the building, bounding up the stairs, a big horsey grin on her face.

"What are you doing here?" Celia opened the door wide.

"Well, hello to you too," Raven said, stepping inside, wood smoke and sweat trailing along behind her. Alabaster leapt from the bench and bolted out the open door. Breathing hard, Raven leaned her hands on her knees and watched as the cat flew across the white yard and dove into the reeds. "That's right, you go on now, big old scaredy-cat." Laughing, Raven closed the door with a big hand and tugged off her sloppy-wet tennis shoes.

Celia removed a mug from the rack and poured Raven a cup of coffee. "What brings you out so early?"

"Exercisin', Sugar. Every morning…after bugle call, I hit the path."

Celia laughed. "Taps?"

"That's for funerals, Sugar."

"Whatever." Celia set the mug on the table and took a seat.

"Besides peaked, you're lookin' satisfied." Raven winked as she flopped a long leg over the bench. "Ditched us for some lovin', huh?" she said. "Dan's mad as hell. You're lucky Donna showed."

"Donna?" Usually just hearing the dancer's name sent Celia into a defensive tirade. But nothing seemed to upset her this morning. "Something came up," she said, pushing the sugar bowl across the table to her friend.

Raven drew a large hand over her flushed face. "Christ sakes, I fryin' in here. Hot coffee, too." She unzipped her lavender sweatshirt and dropped it onto the bench beside her. "Donna'd swipe your job in a whore's second."

"Dan wouldn't let her." Celia watched her friend's eyebrows lift above her sweat-beaded face. Free of makeup, she decided Raven was as plain as brown paper, but when decked out in rouge, blue eye shadow and sequined eyeliner, she was more beautiful than Nefertiti. "Hey, about the other night—"

"It was nothin'," Raven interrupted.

Celia smiled. "Sorry, I was such a bitch. Star's anniversary got to me big time."

"No prob," Raven said, studying her with wide-open eyes. "Got anythin' to eat? Cravin' grits with butter and salt, you know what I mean?"

"No grits. But I have some cookies." Celia retrieved a bag of Oreos from the cupboard next to the sink. "Something I want to show you," she said, and dropped the package on the picnic table. She thought about whisking back her robe to show Raven her healed scars, but instead, she stuck her hand in Raven's face.

"Jay proposed, no shit?"

"What if I say yes? You know how I am."

Raven shrugged. "He don't need to know about your leisure time." Raven removed a cookie from the package and dipped it into the coffee.

Celia watched her friend devour the soggy Oreo. Fingering the silk of her robe beneath the table, she finally spoke, "I read something about apparitions. It said some folks don't know they're dead, while others do. They're on a mission, you know, trying to make contact with loved ones. So they do stuff, like make noise and turn things cold and…"

"That got somethin' to do with a marriage proposal?"

"Well, it's like this…." Celia stood up and opened her robe, revealing the flawless skin of her thighs.

"Where'd your scars go, Sugar?"

Celia's eyes misted over. "Star was in the woods—that's why I wasn't at work last night. She did this."

"What?" Raven leaned onto her elbows, looking hard across the table at Celia's unmarked thighs. "I thought you went AWOL cause you two were doin', you know, the nasty." She laughed nervously.

Celia's frowned, closing up her robe again. She sat back down, feeling wobbly in her being. "I told you, I saw Star on the water. And again, last night in the woods." Celia's eyes misted again. She dabbed them with her napkin. "She was this amazingly brilliant light. I was…."

"Shit, girl." Raven ran a hand over her face, shaking her head. She opened her mouth to speak, but just stammered, "What, where?"

"On my way to work I got lost. I never get lost in the woods. But suddenly, I didn't know where the hell I was. Then this bright light appeared, so bright it lit up the whole forest," Celia said, her eyes watering again. "At first I thought I was almost to work and seeing the club lights." Celia leaned forward conspiratorially. "Then, this icy fog rolled in."

Raven's face turned serious. "Sure it wasn't some jerk-off pullin' a fast one. I warned you, Sugar."

"It was Star." Celia nodded at the sunny glare streaming through the windows. "Her light was brighter than that. She talked to me, Raven. I heard her plain as you're speaking to me now."

Raven raised her eyebrows. "What'd she say, Sugar?"

"Something about me remembering what happened when we were kids. I don't know what she meant by that."

Raven shook her head. "You better quit drinkin' so much, girl."

"I wasn't drunk. I was completely on my game," she said, tears misting her eyes. "Then she was gone. I crouched in the dark for a long time, and then I got scared. So I got up and ran home. I fell in the shale and sliced up my knees and hands."

Raven watched as Celia turned up her left palm and ran a finger over its smooth surface. "My hands and knees were bleeding when I got home. You know where my lifeline used to break," she held out her left hand, "remember? Now it goes clean through. Jay was going to take me to the emergency room."

"Sheez, girl." Raven got up from the bench and walked to the window. "It's the Virgin. I've heard of Mother Mary appearin' in a halo of bright light." She turned back from the window. "What'd she look like? Was she holdin' baby Jesus? Did you smell roses?"

"It wasn't the Virgin." Celia's voice turned low. "It was Star. I even smelled violets. My sister told me to remember what happened." She shook her head. "I've been trying all morning to remember, but my childhood is a blank."

"The cards…."

"What?"

"I saw you fallin'. Better take care, Sugar? I don't want you gettin' hurt."

Celia turned to the woodstove. "See the fire poker there? Jay grabbed it and ran outside, going after the perp. Of course, he came back empty-handed. And when he saw my scars were gone, he bolted. I had the Monroe Miracle, Raven. The frickin' Monroe Miracle."

"Perp's probably still out there hidin' in the reeds." Raven grinned, tapping her acrylic fingernails against the ceramic mug. "Get dressed, Sugar. I wanna take a look around."

Outside, black clouds thickened along the horizon. To the north, ground fog collected in low places below the ridge. Raven watched lily pads bobbing in the bitter wind. She zipped her sweatshirt to just below her chin and jogged in place, waiting for Celia. At least the sun was out. Turning back, she looked at the churchhouse, watching for her friend. She kicked at the hail-clumped reeds. "What's takin' so long?"

Until she'd joined the Army and moved to Vinegar Valley, she thought catfish and sloe gin made life worth livin'. And, of course, Bobby! And then Bobby turned real sour, like the pie cherries ripening out back of Mama's place. When she set off from Vinegar Valley and arrived at her family home in Mississippi, the pit bull next door barked the entire time she and Bobby walked to the river and back. Raven had just opened the gate when her mama stepped out the back door, the Ace of Spades clutched in her right hand. Her face contorted and she dropped dead in a heap at the bottom of the stairs. "Mama!"

Raven shuddered remembering her scream. She bent and picked up a handful of hail and pounded it into a ball. She flung it as far out over the lake as she could.

There was the cremation and then the funeral: bleak and black and muggy beneath southern hat veils. Everyone looked on, judging the sinister family's magic beads hanging from trees in the yard, the spindles on the porch, and cards spread out on the table. She'd brought the cards with her to Vinegar

Valley in Mama's worn velvet bag, but she left the incense behind, except for the smell of bacon grease that is, clinging to her clothes. Everyone thinks the scent is some sweet perfume she wears. She just grins, saying how she polishes the woodstove with bacon grease most every morning—just like Mama always did.

She looked back at the churchhouse once again and drew her hand over her face. Her skin felt gritty with sweat. She needed a good masque to shrink her pores. In the army, pores mattered little; neither did eye shadow and moisturizer. Moisturizer didn't do much good anyway, since the cold wind and hot sun dried you like a biscuit no matter what. When it got really bad, catfish oil was the only thing that healed cracked skin.

She blew into her hands. For some reason, she remembered falling down the day Mama died, banging up her knees, getting up in a rage and slugging Bobby in the jaw. There was this snap and a sharp pain zinged up her arm. Her hand ached for days. Then the paramedics came and tried to revive Mama but instead, took her to the morgue. And then the police came and fined Raven for slugging Bobby in the jaw. After that, she returned to Vinegar Valley and worked as a security guard until the stripping job came along.

At last, Celia stumbled out the door and skidded down the path toward her. Raven grinned wide at her friend. She really did love that girl, even though she was always waiting on her. She hated waiting.

"Smells like spring out here," Celia said. She walked past Raven and headed down the icy path toward the lake.

Raven took in the landscape; the sparkling water, though blue and cold, looked inviting—but the ridge of black clouds forming on the horizon told her the valley would be blinded by snow before nightfall. "Wait up, Sugar."

Celia scooted down the path, slipping through thick spots of hail pocked with footprints. Raven hurried to catch up with her, remembering her mama's words. "Mama used to say that when the dead fail to meet Jesus, they terrify the livin' for the rest of their days. Not out of meanness, of course, just tryin' to get some attention."

Shivering, Raven imagined Star stranded between the layers of matter and spirit. Her mind drifted to the funeral. Her eyes turned to the ground. She recalled the preacher raging around the fire and almost colliding with Celia, who'd stopped to watch a thin curl of smoke lift from the chimney.

"You know," Celia said, "those noises I've been hearing around the house? You said it was the woodstove. JJ said it was the wind. But I think it's been Star all along."

Raven's eyes followed the smoke drifting from the chimney, flowing over the roof and off toward the orchard. A funny feeling stirred in the pit of her stomach. "Maybe you're right, Sugar. Maybe you're right."

CHAPTER EIGHT

Wind gusted, buffeting the car sideways as Celia turned onto Canopy Lane. She pulled up in front of Jay's apartment and shut off the engine. Her bloodied jeans were evidence of her injury. She'd folded them neatly and placed them inside a plastic bag in the bedroom closet. Proof, just in case she needed it when she told Daddy about the miracle.

Celia closed her fingers over her fresh palms. Raven and she had scoured the woods for over an hour and hadn't found a single charred pine needle or trampled maple leaf or muddy footprint. Once she thought she'd heard something, a faint tinkling, like an angel's song, but Raven nixed the idea. Said it was just hail dripping from the trees. But then Raven had kicked at the dirt and reached down, digging under the leaves with her long fingers. She pulled from beneath leaf molder a delicate necklace and handed it to Celia. It was Star's half-heart, lost long ago when Star and Celia had hiked into the forest for a picnic. Once back home, Celia washed the necklace off and put it on, completing the heart that rested at her collarbone.

She needed time to understand everything that had happened, but then there was Jay's reaction and her desire to connect with him around the Monroe Miracle. Plus, she had dance practice later that night. Celia sighed heavily as she climbed out of the car and headed up the stairs leading to his apartment.

Jay's mannerisms lately had been nervous, a foot kicking incessantly, fingers tapping whatever surface he could find to strum. The last time he'd visited, Celia had noticed him looking around at the walls, getting up, sitting down, thinking he'd heard something outside and grabbing his coat before going out to take a look. He'd taken a leave of absence after the shooting, but still couldn't sleep soundly or sit still for very long, so he went back to work.

Then there were the fights; Jay pressing Celia for information. Where had she been? Who was she with? And there were the nights in bed when they were all hot for each other, and suddenly Jay would turn cold and roll away. She took it personally, even though he said that the shrink had advised her not to. He was still grieving. Be patient with him.

She looked up the stairwell to the entrance of JJ's second story apartment. His landlord was remiss: paint chipped and peeling, a loose gutter, and there was a crack in one of the downstairs windows. Just last week, the toilet broke. Instead of calling the landlord, Jay fixed it himself. He was just that way—even if Celia reminded him of who's responsibility something like that was—he'd rather do it himself.

Being a police officer's wife could be interesting, she guessed. There'd be other wives who'd experienced bad things; perhaps incidents like Larry's, an errant shot fired in a dark alley downing a beloved officer, a high-speed chase and crash permanently injuring someone's husband, or something small, like tampering with evidence and jail time. There'd be shared grief, but good things too: baby and wedding showers, Christmas ornament parties, and cocktail hours. As she started up the stairs, she thought, *Yes, cocktail hours. That could be fun!*

"The question is," the captain had said, "can you still be a team player?"

"Yes, Sir," Jay had replied, clasping his hands behind his back, standing at attention. He watched his captain shuffle through paperwork piled high on his desk.

Frowning, the captain nodded, "Okay, then. Follow the rules so I don't have to lay you off. You're on probation now—best I can do. And," he handed him a prescription scribbled on a sheet of paper, "mandatory grief counseling."

The TV blared. It was halftime. Jay had zoned out, resting back in the duct-taped recliner, smelling his own stink and the sourness of spilt beer. Larry's funeral was far behind him and so were the hearings. The ruling: accidental shooting. He rubbed a big hand over his two-day stubble.

He tried to focus on the marching band while finishing off his third beer, enough to numb him; a reprieve from his guilt, but not enough to get him shitfaced. He'd shot and killed his own partner. Now he was stuck with that stupid fuck, Johnny. He swigged the rest of the lukewarm Buck and crushed the can between his fingers. Two weeks ago, he thought he was getting it together. That's why he'd bought the ring for Ceal. He was ready to move forward; ready for the two of them to start a life together.

"Keeping it together," the shrink said, "isn't the goal. The goal is to grieve. It's the only way through to the other side."

"Grief," Jay hissed, feeling his jaw pop with the word. Around town, he'd gotten the reputation as a hothead. Hotheads took chances. Chances were okay, but not if you hadn't cleared your surroundings. He kicked aside a beer can, landing it on the pile of towels and T-shirts he'd pulled from the dryer earlier and left on the floor to fold. The thought crossed his mind; he'd better clean up the place. Never knew when.... Just then, a knock rattled the door.

When Jay returned from the bathroom where he'd washed his pits and changed into a clean T-shirt, Celia was wiping down the kitchen counter. A pot of coffee perked on the stove. He scooped up the pile of T-shirts and towels and carried them into the bedroom. Once Celia and he were hitched, she'd take care of folding laundry. For now, her job was to talk to *frickin' ghosts* and whatever else she did at the club at night, God forbid he ask.

"Okay, then," he said, leaning in to kiss her forehead. "Why the surprise visit?"

Frowning, she took a seat on the bar stool. "I had the Monroe Miracle," she said. "And then you walked out on me." She leaned on the counter and rubbed her palms together. "I needed your support. Instead, I was left alone with what happened in the woods."

Jay took a seat opposite her. Clearing his throat, he said, "Let's see those sainted palms again."

She reached her hands across the kitchen counter, tilting them to the right to catch the brightness from the overhead light. He drew a calloused fingertip over Celia's healthy skin. He'd seen the cuts, bloody and jagged, and was even ready to take her to the hospital for stitches, but she was right, he didn't want to acknowledge the miracle. Sure, Christmas was coming, but that didn't account for the miracle. And miracles were so Biblical, saintly even. He looked up, studying her makeup-free eyes. Even *au naturel*, Celia was hardly a saint. Though, she was lovely.

"JJ?" Celia said.

"Huh?" He smiled weakly.

"I could use some support here."

"Sorry. I've been a little preoccupied." Jay thrummed his fingers deliberately over the clean counter. "It's just that…well, you know. It's weird. Ghosts and disappearing scars. I mean…I'm not used to things like that."

They were quiet for some time, long enough to make Jay feel uncomfortable. He got up from the stool and poured two cups of coffee. In the background, the din of the TV drew his attention. He walked over to the set and turned it off. "When do we help the preacher winterize his church?" he said. "Tomorrow?"

"Yes, at nine." She twisted the engagement ring around her finger. "If you want me to marry you, JJ, you'll need to take me as I am."

He didn't want to argue about how Celia would behave as a cop's wife. He took her hand again and stroked her smooth palm. "How'd you get those scars on your thighs anyway?"

Celia turned away.

"Hey," he said, lifting her chin toward him. "You've never told me. You want me to take you as you are, then I need to know who you are."

"They're cigarette burns," she said, studying the surface of her coffee.

His mind jumped to the interrogation room, the dodgy criminals, the hardened ones, the ones who could look a guy straight in the eye and lie their heads off. "You got a secret, Ceal? Something I should know?"

"No," she said, shaking her head.

"If you do, it's time to fess up."

She took a sip of coffee and looked up, meeting his dark eyes. "I burn myself sometimes to stop the bone pain."

"Sheez! That's fucking nuts!"

"That's supportive!"

"Sorry, I just don't understand."

"It makes me feel better in a weird sort of way."

Jay watched from the doorway as Celia descended the stairs. At the bottom she turned and called back up to him, "See you later."

He nodded, watching as she climbed into her car, pulled out from the curb and drove into the gray day. Weighty clouds sopped the sky, warning him that it was inevitable, that the coming blizzard was going to flatten them.

He stepped back inside and closed the door, deciding he'd blown it with Celia once again. He'd tried to do what the *fag* therapist called *the work*, but when the nagging pain was too much for him to bear, he kept the safety on. He'd hang out in his duct-taped recliner, drinking cheap beer and watching hours of TV, letting everything turn to chaos around him.

When he was with Celia, he felt good, at least better. She was hurting too, he could see the pain in her eyes, and it wasn't just about losing Star. There was tightness in her jaw, and what a jaw it was, angular with just enough width to make her face look exotic. And that black hair of hers killed him. He loved twining his fingers through her curls. When she was sitting at the counter drinking coffee, her beauty overwhelmed him. Even with the game rasping in the background—yeah, he wanted to watch it—there was no comparison. Even when the crowd roared over a field goal, he had to get up and turn the TV off.

The night before, Officer "America" said they'd need to learn to trust each other. Fuckin-A! Sounded like the counselor quipping: *Use smart self-care, Officer Johnson.* But then, he'd fuckin' walked out on Celia. What an ass!

He looked at his watch. He wanted his oasis, his comforting lake of warmth, and he wanted it now. He imagined her long legs wrapping his waist, the growing heat, bliss about to carry him away. That's all he had, a moment of relief. He wanted the feeling again and again. So, he dove for the pearl at the bottom of the murky water and she didn't really seem to mind. Did she?

The phone rang. Jay couldn't move, just sat glued to his chair, his mind clinging to blankness. The phone continued to ring as he waggled a foot, which his therapist said was a nervous habit, something he wanted him to become aware of. "Awareness!" the therapist said, and twirled his pen. "Faggot," Jay mumbled.

And whenever he rolled his eyes, the queer wrote on his chart. "Give me that," he said the other day and grabbed the clipboard out of his hands. He couldn't read the chicken scratch and slammed the notes back on the therapist's desk, fuming. The therapist picked it up and continued taking notes.

He knows what it's like to shut a stove down too far—creosote collects in the sleeve, the collar, the stack. Today the therapist pounced on him when he drifted, his mind floating off to the darkness between Celia's thighs. *It's crazy. I'm crazy, that's it, everyone knows Officer Johnson, JJ is crazy. Jay Johnson, crazy fuckin' nut-case, kills his partner and then a goddamn fag tells me to keep a journal. A journal of his fuckin' namby-pamby feelings.* The phone rang again. Jay rocketed from his chair to answer it. No one was there.

CHAPTER NINE

Celia'd been heaving on lug nuts for the past forty-five minutes. She walloped the flat with the tire iron. "Dammit," she said. Rain plastered her hair to her scalp and streamed down her neck, soaking her silk blouse beneath her winter coat. She looked around. "Where's help when you need it?" Cursing, she watched her breath cloud in the frigid air before her. She jammed the tire iron onto the fourth nut and jumped onto the metal crossbar. Like a kid on a pogo stick, she sprang off the iron, landing a foot away on her rear in a puddle. Moaning, she cursed the sky and its deluge that was now turning to sleet. She got to her feet and turned, seeing a police cruiser barreling toward her. Celia finished brushing off her coat just as the car pulled in behind hers.

"Boy, am I glad to see you," she said as the officer climbed out, wrestling on a green rain-poncho as he walked her way. "Tire's flat and I can't budge the lug nuts."

"You're soaked, Miss," he said, rain dripping off the edges of the poncho hood onto his rosy cheeks. "Go ahead, get in the cruiser. I'll take care of this."

Celia ran over to the car and climbed in. Shivering, she listened to the sleet drumming the roof. Across the road, maple leaves flattened over wet pasture, blurring red to orange through the wet window. The sleet fell harder, now with a bit of snow mixed in. She guessed the weather forecasters were right, there'd be a berm of white stuff blocking her driveway by morning. When she looked back, the officer had become nothing but a grey-green blur hunched over her back tire.

The radio scratched on about pursuits and units and other things that Celia couldn't quite make out over the din of the weather. She was about to turn the volume up when the officer's face appeared in the driver's window. He smiled broadly. She returned the smile. Drenched, he climbed in, smelling of exhaust and wet wool, the mix reminding her of a sleazy hotel room out off the highway.

"I hate being so helpless," she said, and brought her fingers to her throat, drawing them downward toward the neck of her wet shirt, feeling the chain with the completed heart resting at the base of her throat. At first, Celia couldn't remember where she'd put her half, but then she'd found it in her underwear drawer.

The officer looked away. "Someone over-tightened that last lug nut," he said. "It's nothing you did wrong." He switched the fan on high. "Warming up? One thing good about a squad car, the heaters really can dish it out." The officer wiped his forehead with a handkerchief, brushing brunette curls aside. His rosy cheeks were closely-shaven, giving him a look of vulnerability. She continued to stroke her neck as she studied him.

The officer tipped his head. "You look familiar."

Shrugging, she stuck out her hand. "Celia Monroe."

"Monroe? Oh, you're Star's twin." He grabbed her hand and shook it hard. "You probably don't remember me. I'm Johnny. I took your sister to the senior prom. Sorry to hear about…."

Celia looked down, pulling her hand away. She glanced up, trying to put his current face with the baby face she recalled from that night so long ago; a boy in a black tux wearing a ruffled shirt and tart aftershave. Once again, she felt the pain of loss knife her gut. Now Johnny's chin was square and his eyes were heavy lidded and long lashed. Celia had stayed home with the flu that night, watching from the hall as Star repeatedly hiked up the blue strapless number to keep it from slipping off her stick-thin figure. She remembered Star's sky-blue eyes closing when she brought the carnation corsage to her nose to smell. She looked like an angel.

"You look just like her," Johnny said. "Except you're dark coloring." He cleared his throat. "I don't go by Truman anymore, it's America now."

"America?" Celia laughed. "Why?"

"It's a long story."

"Oh," Celia said, and turned to the window. Big flakes had begun collecting at the sides of the windshield where the defroster wasn't working. "I'm sure it is. So, you're JJ's new partner. I'm his girl, did you know that?"

"Jay's girl?" the officer said, raising his eyebrows. "Nope, I didn't." He shifted in his seat, fastening the seatbelt around his hips. "I'll follow you to the station," he said. "Make sure that tire holds."

Celia grinned. "Thanks, Johnny," she said, and opened the door.

"Star's smile," he said.

"Star's gone," Celia said. "This is my smile." She climbed out of the rig into the falling snow.

Snow fell harder now and the roads turned slick. Celia tightened her hands on the steering wheel. In the rearview mirror she could see the cruiser following her at a safe distance. She imagined Officer America removing his shirt and unbuckling his gun belt, stepping naked toward her, eyes dark and penetrating. Tingles warmed her body. Surely there was a Bible verse about flesh and spirit being one that would rationalize her making this kind of mistake once again. She bit her lip hard, knowing that God would want her to be free. However, Daddy would advise God's lamb not to enter into temptation. And JJ would be devastated. But, if she played her cards right, neither would find out how she actually conducted her life.

Tingles turned into a shiver. It was cold outside and her clothing was damp. She turned the heater up. While waiting for the tire repair, she'd walk across the street to Peggo's Grill and order coffee with a shake of cayenne and splash of heavy cream. "Hmmm," she said, imagining the warm cup clasped between her hands. "Sounds like a cure-all."

At the edge of town, she slowed, passing the boarded up café where she and Star had ordered cocoa with marshmallows melting white and sticky across the top. They were just kids then. Now she preferred heavy cream swirling into patterns over bitter black. Maybe Johnny would join her for a cup.

Pumping her brakes, she slid a little, gained control again, turning slowly into the garage parking lot. She parked next to the garage doors and set the emergency brake. Behind her, the cruiser's headlights reflected in her rearview mirror. It was dusk and the falling snow brightened in the headlights like Star's glow in the woods.

Celia shut off the engine and stepped into the plume of exhaust lifting heavenward from Johnny's car. The weather forecaster said the white stuff would mount to fourteen inches by morning. And she was expected at the club tonight. Dan would keep the club open no matter what. Then there was the Donna thing. Getting there would be fine, but she'd be hard-pressed to walk home at three in the morning, all sweaty from swinging her hips, bracing herself against a blinding blizzard. She'd need a ride.

Officer America climbed out of the cruiser, his rain poncho rustling as he walked across the parking lot. "Tim will fix you up. Drive safely on your way home."

"Thanks for your help," Celia said. "Really, I appreciate it."

"It's my job." Nodding, he turned toward Peggo's Grill and strode off.

Snow tinted pink as it fell in front of the red chili pepper sign lighting the restaurant's steps. Celia watched Johnny walk through the falling flakes. He waited for a car to pass, turning back once to give her a nod. She waved then turned to the garage where the sound of the air gun made her jump.

"May I help you miss?" Tim Sergeant of Sergeant's Garage stood just inside the open garage door, wiping his hands on a grease rag.

"Yeah, I had a flat out on Route 60. Can you fix it?"

"Cilantro colors the tortillas, you know, green and then the flavors mix, tasting like the forest smells." Celia smiled. "Other dishes are very hot, Tex-Mex style. So hot you can't taste anything but the heat. Some hate hot and others love it. Take my dancer friend, Kiki. She does 5 stars and then blots her forehead with a tissue. Me, well, 2 stars is fine, except for when I'm feeling spunky, then 3 stars is better. Star couldn't take the heat at all."

Johnny nodded and continued to eat as Celia rattled on. Celia smiled, feeling like a jabbering idiot. A fine mist of sweat had risen along her upper lip. She looked down, wiping her mouth with a napkin. When she looked up again, Johnny had turned to the window, which was condensing with big drips that rolled down the glass, puddling onto the sill. He reached out with his napkin and wiped the sill dry.

Outside, three inches of snow blanketed the cars lined up in front of the diner. Across the street, the garage was dark. Tim had been called out to pull ditch-divers back onto the road. He wouldn't get to her car until Tuesday. He'd offered to give her a ride home, but she had declined. She had something better in mind.

Johnny turned back, nodding to someone beyond where Celia was sitting across from him. Celia looked around. It was the waitress, Mary Beth, from high school, better known as "That Slut Who Stole My Boyfriend." She no longer ratted her hair up high in front and her makeup wasn't so garish now. She walked out from behind the counter with a plate of food and headed their way. Several guys turned to check her out, but no one drooled, since she was clearly six months along.

"Here you go," Mary Beth said, and set the plate of tortillas before Celia.

"Thanks," Celia said, watching the waitress walk off. From behind she didn't look pregnant at all. Celia sat forward in the booth. "She's not married, you know."

Johnny cleared his throat. He was taking a break from the heat, gulping water before continuing to plow through the pileup of burritos and the mudslide of frijoles. Celia dove into her honey drizzled fried tortillas sprinkled with cayenne, feeling happier than she had in a long time.

"Seems like she should be," he finally said.

Celia nodded, her mouth on fire: "The Fireline" they called it at Peggo's Grill. She had more than one *fire line* to deal with, the latest being set by Johnny.

"So, your car is ready to go?" Johnny said.

"Not until Tuesday. Tim got called out—crashes all over the place. Can you drop me at home?"

"Lake Monroe still?"

Celia nodded. "Same ol' little churchhouse. Daddy and Mama no longer live there. Just me."

"That's my beat." Johnny smiled and pushed his plate away. Again, he turned to watch the snow falling outside. He shook his head, "Gonna be a long night."

Celia studied his curls and long lashes, admiring his strong chin, his smoothly shaven cheeks. When he turned back, she looked away. An awkward silence and then fortunately, the waitress (maybe slut still applied) showed up with coffee and the bill. Mary Beth smiled sweetly as she poured Johnny's refill but refrained from looking at Celia as she topped off her coffee. Celia thanked her and poured in some cream and a shake of chili pepper.

"Delicious," she smiled, certain her desire for Johnny would demand that the Bible be hidden beneath the bed.

"I'll get it," Johnny said and left to pay the bill. She turned and watched him standing at the cash register. He smiled at the waitress, then turned and looked back at her.

Snowflakes split over the grill of the police car like water over a diver. Somehow the sight reminded Celia of Star brightening the forest with her angelic light. Star's directive was that Celia must remember; however, she didn't know what she was supposed to remember. Maybe JJ could help her figure it out, but then again, he didn't buy the story of Star's visitation. Even with proof of the miracle—her flawless skin—he was disinclined to believe in such things.

The snow was already freezing on the road, causing the cruiser to slide at the stop sign. Celia jammed her feet into the floorboards as they headed into the intersection. Finally, Johnny let off on the brake and coasted through. "Good thing I'm the law," he laughed.

The radio squawked. Johnny grabbed the handset, answering in his cop voice. Celia suddenly felt sick. If she got caught having a fling with this man it would surely break JJ's heart, yet at the same time her energy felt as unstoppable as that icy slide through the intersection.

The cruiser rounded a corner onto the highway. She grabbed the door handle to keep from falling into Johnny. Just past the shoulder, she could see through the falling flakes, the neighbor's abandoned chicken coop had collapsed. Celia remembered hitting those chickens with a stick when she was a little kid. Daddy had run after her, shouting, "How'd you like *me* to take a stick to *your* backside?" She'd shot off into the orchard, her daddy at her heels. He didn't catch her that time.

The speaker squawked again. Johnny mumbled cop-talk that made no sense, until he said *over and out*. He clipped the mic back onto the set. "Officer Jay and I were supposed to meet out at Firing Range Road tonight, but Captain Bailey's keeping me in town. Driving separate, we'll be able to cover more territory."

"It's so dark out there," Celia said, imagining JJ in a panic. "Makes me worry." She felt sick again and sank down in the seat, resting her head against the seatback. Her ring flashed beneath the glow of the dash lights. She covered it with her right hand.

Johnny slowed the cruiser to a crawl, the windshield already buried. The wipers compressed the white stuff into wedges along either side of the glass. He turned to her, his face looking pinched in the dimness. She could smell him in the heated air, his sweat and the lingering scent of Tex-Mex on his clothes. "Just ahead, then?"

"Yeah," she said, "Past the turnoff to the Sanitarium." She sat up, feeling the sickness draining into her pelvis as they neared her driveway. The flying flakes made it difficult to see. She couldn't tell where the edge of the road ended and the ditch began. Reaching out a hand, she touched Johnny's sleeve. "I'm scared," she said.

"It's just snow," Johnny laughed. "Up ahead, there on the right, isn't it?"

"Yeah!"

Johnny tapped the brakes. The patrol car moved into a slide, heading toward the mailboxes. He turned the wheel to the left, continuing to tap the brakes. The cruiser slid toward the ditch. Celia gasped. Johnny spun the wheel the opposite direction. The front fender moved right, smashing into the mailbox, dropping the front tire into the ditch, tossing them both forward. Celia caught herself with both hands against the dash.

"You okay?" Johnny said.

"Fine," she said, watching him press the shift lever into reverse. "Forgot to warn you about the shoulder. Caved in the last hard rain we had. Soft earth there by the mailbox."

Turning, Johnny swung his arm over the seat back. Behind them everything was white except for pink exhaust drifting through the taillights. "Let's see what she's got," he said, revving the engine, spinning the tires in an attempt to back out of the ditch. Tires whirred and the police car settled, remaining planted.

The blowing snow streaked past the streetlight, whisking over the pine copse toward the lake. Johnny flung an arm around Celia and together they leaned into the wind, trudging down the long driveway toward the churchhouse. His heft steadied her, but the blizzard's sting to her cheeks reminded her of the wintery night she'd walked home from the club and found her mother standing in her closet, lifting an ash-coated finger to her colorless mouth.

"My dead sister," Celia had said. "How could you?" She'd grabbed the urn out of her mother's hands and set it back on the shelf. It was afterward that they checked her mama into the sanitarium.

"Where's the woodpile?" Johnny shouted. "I'll bring in a few armloads."

The wind blasted around the corner, stealing Celia's breath. She relinquished his support and pointed to the back. "Come inside when you're done," she shouted, stomping up the porch steps to the door.

Johnny had a monumental shoveling job ahead of him. *He'll need warmth and a drink,* she thought, turning the key in the lock and stepping inside. Celia switched on the lights, catching a whiff of tortillas and peppers wafting from beneath her coat as she hung the snowy garment on the wall hook. She toed-off her snow-clumped boots and stepped into slippers. The house was still warm even though the fire had died down. She opened the woodstove and a gust of wind puffed a curl of smoke into the kitchen. She stuffed in newspaper and several sticks of applewood and closed the door partway.

She poured two glasses of wine, one for herself and one for Johnny. After a few swallows, the jitters in her stomach settled into flowing warmth. Shortly, flickering flames and snapping wood cheered the room and she knew that when Johnny came inside with a load of wood, she'd offer him the rocker by the fire.

Jay always grumbled when he stacked wood. She imagined his furled brow, his hard-set jaw. By now he was probably inching along the highway, windshield wipers snapping, visibility less than poor. Out past the firing range, the weather always worsened, and while searching for GIs who'd gotten too cocky and careened into a ditch, many a cop had ended up in trouble as well. Celia was surprised Jay wasn't one of the crazies being hauled out of a ditch after all those Bucks he'd downed earlier. Hopefully her pot of coffee had helped sober him up.

"In some ways Johnny's more my type," she said, stripping off her wet clothing. She hung the damp items on the back of the bathroom door, listening all the while for the *thud, thud, thud* of logs hitting the porch. "Serve and protect," she said, hurrying. Suddenly, she wanted him like she wanted the wine, like she wanted the cigarette burn, like she wanted her sister back. She tied on her red silk robe and applied a fresh coat of *Rascal Red.*

She didn't know what her daddy would think of the miracle, but she knew what he'd think of her cheating on JJ. Copulating out of wedlock, no matter whom she did it with, was a sin. She shrugged, thinking of all those Christians she'd be letting down. Her daddy's opinion didn't really matter to her that much, although the thought of him judging her sent a creepy-crawly feeling up her spine.

The door banged open. "Celia?" Johnny cleared his throat. "Celia, you there?"

"Just a minute," she called.

"I'm heading out," Johnny called. "Got everything you need?"

Wait," she said, and checked her image in the mirror. She stepped into the hall.

There stood Johnny, all red-cheeked and covered in snow. His eyebrows shot up when he saw her draped in silk. He looked at the floor, embarrassed. He turned, reaching for the door. Behind him, out on the highway, a transformer blew. The explosion sent sparks into the sky, lighting everything to daylight before swallowing the valley and the little church-house in complete darkness.

CHAPTER TEN

When Celia was young, she had no interest in sleeping around; in fact, her stomach jittered when guys pulled her in for a kiss or a pet, and sometimes she'd even freeze in place until they stood back and said, "Whatever!" and took her home. It was embarrassing to act so stupidly.

Now the pursuit and possible conquest of a sexy guy turned her into a cat in heat. Celia frowned. Johnny was already out the door by the time she'd said, "Wait." Could she blame him, being Jay's partner and all, standing there in her silk robe?

She felt her way to the matches and struck one. She lit a candle. Shivering, she lit two more. The ticking started, this time the sound seemed to come from the room above. Light flickered across the attic door. For some reason the jumping shadows had her standing at the top of the stairs in her memory. She was a young girl, listening hard, but for what?

Her stomach dropped. Was that what Star meant? Was there something important she'd forgotten from her childhood? She tapped her forehead with her palm, thinking hard until her brain seized up. "Enough," she said, and walked to the counter to refill her glass.

Curling into the rocker, she pulled the throw around her shoulders. Outside, the wind howled, blowing wet clumps of snow against the windows. Celia couldn't help but think that Johnny would have crawled into her bed if she'd said the right word; in fact, she was sure of it. Wine took the edge off her loneliness, but still the desire for a cigarette yanked her insides forward. Sighing, she ran fingertips over her smooth thighs, intrigued still by their newborn smoothness.

Johnny was ethical, that was more than she could say for herself. A thoughtful guy; not at *all* like Jay with all his angst and strictly enforced rules. Johnny's twinkling eyes said he found her charming. But there was something secretive about him, too; yes…that was it! The ticking continued, though it had lessened.

She sipped her wine, letting Johnny's curls and hooded eyes swim through the fuzziness of her buzz. Absently, she touched the engagement ring; surely Johnny wouldn't want someone as despicable as her for a girlfriend.

A volley of snow spattered the windows, startling her. Every time a blizzard blew through Vinegar Valley, the power went out. The candles lined up on the picnic table burned hot, dripping wax down the sides of the tapers. Her eyes found the flickering light mesmerizing. She leaned her head against the chair back and stared drowsily at the flicking flames.

Like the lake, she'd changed one day; everything that was calm up to that point turned rough. Her lust charged forth out of control. Yes, she'd even tried to kiss old farts; anything that walked upright and smelled remotely male was fair game.

The phone rang. Celia stumbled from the rocker and across the room to the counter. She lifted the receiver. "Hello?"

"Ceal, thank goodness the phone's working."

"JJ, where are you?"

"Some farmer's house," Jay said. "Spun out. My rig's smashed against the bank on Skeet Road. Broken axle."

"Good God, are you all right?"

"Shaken and wet. That putz, Johnny, never showed. Maybe he's in a ditch somewhere. Could you call…."

"Precinct wants him on patrol in town tonight." Celia twisted the phone cord around her hand. "I had a blowout after I left your place, JJ. He happened by and gave me a ride into town."

"Shit, I was going to fix that," Jay said. "Sorry, Ceal. Is it taken care of?"

"Not until tomorrow. Swamped, you know, the storm and all."

"Sure, sure," Jay said, lowering his voice. "Hey, I got to thinking, you know the Larry thing?"

"No, JJ." Celia pressed the receiver closer to her ear.

"Listen, Celia…I fired my gun yesterday. I didn't tell you because, well," he said. "It's the first time since…."

"JJ, you weren't supposed to have it on you."

"I fired while the train was passing. The noise, man, it was deafening, and the wind and train, shit…it changed me."

"JJ, I'm worried about you." Celia bit her lip. "You know what the shrink said."

"I'm fine, now. Better than ever. Really!"

The phone cord twisted tighter around Celia's hand. "JJ, your partner's out on the road digging out his rig."

"What? Sheez, he's a moron."

"His front tire slid into the ditch by the mailbox. I'll tell him to pick you up, if I see him."

"Tell him I'm east of the tracks. Smith's place, 328-3919."

Celia scribbled down the number. "Okay."

"Be safe, Ceal."

"Night, JJ. Love you." She hung up the receiver and sighed a long, tired sigh.

Pop, pop, pop. Celia startled at the sound of applewood flaring in the woodstove. Clearing her head, she realized it wasn't the wood, someone was knocking at the door. Through the icy glass, a blurred figure stood hunched against blowing snow. Jumping up, she stumbled across the kitchen, her hand shaking as she opened the door. A blast of snow followed Johnny inside.

"Cruiser's going nowhere," he said, stomping the snow from his boots. "See that, another transformer blew?" He shook the snow from his hair and turned to peer into the darkness. "There," he pointed, "out past the lake. Felt weird out there, like someone was watching."

Celia helped Johnny take off his coat. "There aren't any power poles beyond the driveway," she said, hanging his coat by the door. Celia remembered the brilliance of her sister's light brightening the woods to daylight. She pressed her face against the glass and imagined she could make out a faint glow hovering over the lake. *Star*, she thought and turned back to Johnny, who stood warming his hands over the stove. "I'll run you a hot bath."

"I can't stay," he said, toeing off his boots. "I'll just hang these wet socks over the chair back to dry. You got a spare pair I can borrow?" He dropped onto the footstool and pulled off his socks. "They're expecting me back at the precinct tonight. I'll hitch into town."

Celia handed him a dishtowel to dry his hair. She found a pair of Jay's socks and gave them to him. Then she offered him the glass of wine she'd poured earlier. "Jay called. He wondered where you had gotten to."

"Should be out there dealing with this mess." Johnny took the glass of wine and swallowed it down. "Thanks," he said, wiping his mouth with the back of his hand.

"He's broken down. Called from a farmer's house." Celia nodded at Johnny's snow-crusted pants. "Better hang those over the chair back to dry."

Johnny looked at his watch. When he looked up again, his eyes reflected the candle flames. "I'm still on duty, Celia."

She came up close behind him. "Hard to hitchhike in a blizzard."

He turned, staring down at her with dark eyes.

She knelt down, her fingers finding the zipper of his pants. "Better get out of these wet clothes."

Johnny's fingertips pressed into Celia's trembling back. The same slender fingers that could shove a criminal to the ground, could also gently trace the rise and fall of her silky flesh.

"Johnny," she breathed into his salty neck.

Johnny hardened against her pelvis. "Star," he sighed.

CHAPTER ELEVEN

Star had read stories about folks bending silverware with their thoughts or astral traveling to far off lands, but now she was living proof, rather now she was dead proof, that the veil between physical life and what she called the spirit world, was as sheer as the palest lacewing.

Star sat on the edge of Celia's bed watching Johnny pull on his pants. Oh, how she'd obsessed over him while dusting the aisles of organic peas and honey granola. At the same time she was going boy crazy, she also realized that anyone could walk through walls if they tried. So when a customer wasn't waiting to be checked out, Star flattened her cells and slipped through the lath and plaster next to the cash register, weaving between the molecules of the message-studded bulletin board, passing shelves laden with nasty smelling dried herbs her boss kept in gallon jars, to arrive in cold storage where tofu and raw milk sat in stacked crates and organic vegetables crowded wooden bins. That was where she hovered, taking in the shimmering light emanating from sweet potatoes and peppers, their beauty mesmerizing and somehow enlivening. After the adventure, she returned to the checkout stand and helped a customer purchase a jar of Miracle Energy.

Besides walking through walls, she loved to visit the starry tunnel before falling asleep at night. She once told Johnny about the whoosh of her spirit lifting out the top of her head as she coursed toward the vastness of everything. Sometimes it frightened her, the speed at which her spirit ripped free. Johnny once asked her if anyone ever got stuck out there in the ethers. She replied with what her Spirit guide always said, *Nothing in this vast universe will hurt you, Dear*.

Star wondered if that day in the boat, if she hadn't tried so hard to convince her sister that the preacher was the cause of

Celia's jezebel behavior, would she still be living upstairs. Still be listening to the churchhouse's front door open with a hush, then click lightly closed. Still hear her sister and some guy's footsteps hesitate at the bottom of the stairwell before a muffled thud of the attic door shut out their giggles. As she thought about it, her molecules dimmed. Maybe it wasn't so bad, but really, the last thing she wanted was to hear some jerk yowling like a wildcat in her parents' old bedroom. It was on nights like that, that she would cover her head with the pillow and escape into the tunnel, taking care not to float too close to the glistening light at the end.

Star ran her vaporous fingers over her grandmother's wedding-ring quilt. Everything looked the same—although things sparkled more in the afterlife—even her urn of ashes in the closet shone. Some day she hoped Sissy would dump them in the lake. After all, it had been a year since her watery demise in Lake Monroe. *Long enough*, she thought, *for her twin to move on*.

Johnny came out of the bedroom carrying a candle. Star spiraled through the walls following him into the kitchen, arriving just in time to see Celia, draped in red silk, weaving toward the back door, a full wine glass in hand. Outside a gust of snow spattered the window and the wind howled. Star rattled the stove pipe for added drama. The fire sparked and Celia turned in Star's direction, raising her dark eyebrows curiously. "Wind's pickin' up," she slurred, her free hand covering the back of her neck as Star streamed a cold draft like a scarf circling her. She wanted to get Sissy's attention without frightening her too much, but then there was Johnny approaching her from behind. Emotion streamed around the candlelit room as he set down his taper and wrapped his arms around Celia.

Star ticked across the room. The cat sprang out of the chair and ran into the bedroom. *It will take some figuring out,* Star thought, *this making contact with the living. And with Johnny involved, it would be easier to just slip back through the veil and manifest a sweet life away from this tangled mess.*

Then the idea came to her—maybe she'd bebop over to Daddy's house and see what the old goat was up to. Hopefully snugged beneath a pile of warm covers with a hot water bottle tucked in at his feet. Yes, hot water would last in the tank for a while longer, until the bitter cold outside soaked into everything, that is.

"Keep 'er dripping," Daddy always said. She was sure the old goat would practice what he preached; except he never did when it came to the *thou shalt not* list. And that's what she wanted Celia to remember. The *shalt nots* that Daddy never obeyed.

Star lifted off the table and in a spray of ectoplasm, cartwheeled out through the door into the blizzard, which to her was nothing more threatening than a lovely spring shower. Couldn't they see the camas growing along the lake shore, and all those soft brown reeds, cat-got-your-tongue tails?

Alone in the house, Star could see Johnny hugging Celia. "I was going to give digging out the cruiser one last shot, but on second thought…."

"Jay is still out there," Celia said. "I'm worried about him."

"He's trained for hardship."

"He's a baby, trust me."

In her dream, Celia ran endlessly through the orchard maze, heart pounding fast as she turned this way and that. She spied a turnoff she recognized as the way leading to the lake and little churchhouse. Relief flooded her, but when she stepped through the opening, instead of seeing a familiar landscape, she faced a forest filled with sparking light. Shielding her eyes, she made out Star's form wavering in the brilliance, her luminous fingers beckoning Celia to come closer. Celia gulped, whirling around in the opposite direction, her speed increasing as she ran until she lifted off the ground and flew.

She woke with a gasp, her shins pressed against the back of Johnny's calves. He hadn't moved beneath the pile of warm blankets since he'd said goodnight and turned away. His steady breathing calmed her racing heart. She rolled to the edge of the bed and sat up, placing her feet on the cold floor, steadying herself against the buzz in her head. Maybe her twin was right. Maybe she did have something to remember; maybe something awful had happened to her.

She pulled on her robe and padded down the icy hall to the bathroom. Inside, she lit a candle and used the toilet. She was curious if she could call up her sister like she'd read in the book on communicating with apparitions. Shivering, she finished up and tiptoed down the creaky hall, holding the candle high to light the way to the sanctuary.

The wind howled around the churchhouse, rattling the long row of windows that let the sun inside, illuminating the sanctuary on summer church mornings. At the end of the long room she dropped onto the cushion facing the altar, a place she liked to sit when she felt particularly guilty about her carnal appetites. She set the candle on the floor in front of her and repeated her petition to God for leniency, believing that if she really was as vile as her daddy suggested, any bit of help would be welcome.

The candle flame flickered sideways, nearly extinguishing in a draft. It flickered toward the ceiling again, lengthening its light, dancing shadows across the long wall and the preacher's teetering stacks of hymnals stored in the corner. He'd left them there the day he'd moved Vanessa into their new home. After Star died, his threats about Hell's brimstone became a wall Celia didn't know how to penetrate. She'd seen a vision of her dead sister, for God's sake, and just now had dreamed of the brilliant light that illuminated the orchard. Surely that wasn't the Devil's doing. The Devil didn't wrap God's children in tremendous love only to trick them later, did he? No, she was certain that's not how it worked.

Celia studied the candle flame. "Please, Star," she whispered, "talk to me. I won't run away this time, I promise."

Celia waited, listening to the house creak, the snow steadily ticking against the windowpanes, and the occasional snap of the candle's flame. She cocked her head, half expecting her sister's sweet voice to trickle into the room from between the plaster cracks, but nothing other than the sound of the storm disturbed the quiet.

"Star?" Celia turned to the hymnals again, vowing to take them to the dump as soon as the roads were passable. But instead of her sister, she saw a shadow that resembled the expressionless face her daddy wore the day Star died. As it flickered across the walls, she felt an icy chill deep in her core. She knew that for her father, prayer and obeisance to church business was his salvation; however, to Celia, hiding behind his precious Bible was a behavior no different than Vanessa's stunned silence.

"Star, are you there?" Celia whispered, recalling the ashes tucked away in the back of her closet. Star'd been locked away in a dark void of non-life, non-death for far too long; maybe that's why her twin had returned—Star wanted to be set free.

Star filtered through attic cobwebs, sneaking between wires and wood knots as her vaporous cells trickled through the sanctuary ceiling and settled on top of the candlestick, becoming the blue glow at the base of the flame that flickered before her twin, the beautiful Celia Monroe. Tugging at the knots in her hair, Star whispered, "Good idea, Sissy, set me free in the lake, but then you must set yourself free as well."

Star had tried to explain to her twin why Celia felt so miserable, but only a mournful sound came out of her mouth, causing the candle flame to flicker and nearly go out. Celia cocked her ear toward the window and the howling wind outside. She knew that Celia thought the sound she just made was the winter storm. She desperately wished she could make her twin see through the veil.

"I don't get it, Star. You show yourself to me in the woods, and then you appear in my dreams. Why don't you talk to me? Star…Star, please!" Celia waited, but only the wind startled her. Finally, she gave up. Shivering with cold, she thought of Johnny asleep in her bed, probably dreaming of cruising neighborhoods, driving down one street then another, keeping Vinegar Valley safe from evil. Someone had to do it!

Beyond the edges of the bedroom, Celia imagined Jay sleeping in a spare room at a farmer's house out by the railroad crossing. She knew it would be late morning before he made it back to Lake Monroe. Up on the hill, no doubt the preacher was reading his Bible beneath a pile of wool blankets, a flashlight illuminating all those tiny *Thou shalt nots*…the tip of his nose drippy cold; and at Luna Sanitarium, Vanessa was sitting upright in the darkened room, her mind flat as a pane of glass.

Celia sighed. "Okay, Star. First you go, and then all your stuff goes. And Daddy's old hymnals, well, they're out of here, too." She fingered the silver heart she wore around her neck. "Well, almost everything goes." She lifted the candle, climbed off the cushion and tiptoed back to the bedroom.

The puffs of air leaving Johnny's lips sounded sweet, unlike Jay's snores that could stir, and probably wake any number of specters. And her feelings for Johnny, too, felt different than the feelings she had for Jay. As she watched him sleep, she felt a deep affection for Star's old beau. Oddly, she felt as though she loved him. Celia almost blew out the candle and climbed back into bed, but instead, she set the candle on the dresser and reached through the folds of silk clothing to the back corner of the closet, wrapping her fingers around the cold metal handles of the urn. She lifted it down, the weight of it surprisingly heavy. Star had been frail, but her ashes felt like a bucket of stones. She stood there feeling a bit faint, holding the cold urn against her belly, her head abuzz with wine.

Johnny rolled over in his sleep and the smell of their lovemaking wafted into the chilly air. Its salty scent caused her desire for him to reignite, tingling her spine. Again, she nearly abandoned her mission. But his rig was high-centered out at the road, with snow drifting deeper by the moment. There was nowhere for him to go. She lifted the taper and made her way by the flickering flame into the kitchen.

She placed the urn on the counter and stared at it, trying not to imagine the scene: Star's dead body rolling into the flames for cremation. And then a different sort of horror gripped her: her sister locked away indefinitely in the back of her bedroom closet. How long would Daddy keep her there? Celia shuddered. "I'm releasing you, Star," she said, and grabbed a kitchen knife to pry the lid off the container.

Inside, bone bits peppered the gray ash. She thought of digging through the silty powder, thinking she'd find a silver filing or a crumble of Star's clavicle. She remembered the look her mother had shot her that day: crazy saucer-eyes as black as Alabaster's. "Star's gone," she had said. "Never coming back. She's gone forever. Gone." Then, before Celia's horrified eyes, her mother turned into a comatose pillar.

As Celia touched the ash, a spark snapped against her fingertip like a shorted wire. She drew back, expecting a presence to flow genie-like from the urn and envelop her. She remained utterly still, listening. Another snap. She breathed a sigh of relief. It was just the firewood popping in the stove. Still, Star's grinning face came to mind. It was the summer of sixth grade and Star had escaped the preacher's chores early to join Celia at the lake where they swam out to the giant lilies and crawled out of the water to sun themselves on a log. Celia recapped the urn and pulled on her coat and rubber boots. It was time to take Star for a swim.

CHAPTER TWELVE

Great gusts of wind whipped swirls of snow around Celia's bundled form, stinging her face with icy pricks. Hooded, she lowered her head into the storm and stumbled across the yard, wielding the flashlight with its bobbing beam. "Fuck!" she said, snow spilling into her rubber boots, her silk robe whipping around below the hem of her coat as she staggered across the snowy yard to the boathouse.

She and JJ had secreted away a rowboat two summers ago. He said he wanted to go fishing out beyond the lilies, but she'd shaken her head, knowing how her daddy felt about boats and the tangled roots. "Not there. That's where the monster lives," she'd said, immediately feeling childish for spouting such nonsense. But she went on, reciting the myth that her mother had repeated to the twins often: *There's a lake monster living under the surface, always ready to pull an innocent one beneath.*

Jay smirked, but she went on, "A kid drowned, his legs tangled in lake weed. People still swear that the hoarse cries of the drowned boy can be heard echoing through the valley on particularly dark and lonely nights."

Together they heaved the boat under the boathouse deck to hide it from the preacher's prying eyes. Now she singlehandedly wrestled the rowboat from its hiding place, thankful the deck overhang had kept it dry. Gasping, she pulled and pushed, rocking and dragging it through the snow-covered tules toward the water. Twice, she slipped and fell on her knees and struggled to her feet again, brushing snow from her legs. One more pull and the boat began to float.

Celia splashed into the water, frigid lake sloshing over the top of her boots and soaking her robe and the hem of her coat. She secured the urn beneath the seat. Then she half-stepped, half-fell in the boat, settling herself on the bench seat. She pushed off. Oars secure in the oarlocks, she pulled hard, using her anger at her daddy's constant criticism to fuel her fight against the icy headwind.

What she did or didn't do was none of his business. But Daddy always went a little crazy when it came to the lake. Probably had something to do with her grandfather's near drowning and losing Star to the root-strewn lake bottom. She remembered the day he'd stopped by last fall to check on the apple crop. Celia'd been out taking her morning swim when he'd strode across the yard, shouting at her to immediately remove herself from the Devil's maw. She continued crawling across the lake, swimming toward the lilies as she always did, his flailing shape onshore growing smaller and smaller.

Celia kept her head lowered as she rowed. The wind buffeted the little boat, water breaking against its wooden sides in icy sprays. The day Star drowned, the two of them argued bitterly. That day, the lake roiled as well. She cringed each time she recalled yanking Star's arm, her sister's fall into the lake remaining a bitter stone forever turning in her stomach.

Celia swallowed several times. The wind picked up, shrieking through the trees surrounding Lake Monroe. Celia ducked her head, rowing harder, the flashlight resting on her lap, pointing toward the tangled lily pads. The wooden hull hit a deadhead—the thud muted by the heavy falling snow. The force of the impact tossed Celia to the boat's bottom. Shaken and swearing, she thought she heard the cry of a wounded animal coming from somewhere beyond the surging pads. She crawled back onto the seat, tucked the oar tips inside the boat, and, moving quickly, attempted to pry the metal lid off the urn. Her freezing fingers slipped off the wet sides and the urn nearly flipped into the lake. "Dammit!" Frantically she rubbed her hands over her coat, drying her palms. She continued, working the metal back and forth, until the lid finally clattered to the bottom of the boat.

Celia lifted the heavy urn with frozen hands and swung it sideways. Ash caught in the wind and whipped over the lily pads. Star's ashes sounded like sand spattering the surface of the water. An acidic taste settled over Celia's cracked lips.

She touched her tongue to her upper lip, remembering the natives she'd read about who stirred their loved one's ashes into a cauldron of bubbling yam soup; the whole tribe dining on the dead relative, each swallowing a bit of burnt bone and becoming one with the deceased. Why had she been so shocked when her mother touched her ashy finger to her tongue? Celia shook her head, settling back on the wet seat. "Now I'm part of you, Sissy, just like I'm part of the lake."

A tinkling sound threaded through the snowy air. Hair rose on the back of her neck. She tossed the urn into the lake and gripped the wooden oars, cutting the tips through the water again and again, pulling until her arms burned with exhaustion. The boat finally slammed ashore and Celia leapt from the vessel, dragging it far enough out of the lake to keep it from floating off. Splashing through the shallows, feet frozen inside her rubber boots, Celia followed her disappearing footprints back across the yard and into the little churchhouse.

CHAPTER THIRTEEN

The sun reflected off the snow, stinging Jay's eyes even with his police-issue dark glasses pushed high on his nose. It was an interlude, this sun, for through the windshield he could see the horizon and the black clouds gathering thickly in the west. "More snow on its way," he sighed, his mind turning to the distance in Celia's voice when he'd called the night before. Still mad at him, he supposed, for not believing in her apparition. But that wasn't all his cop-instinct was telling him; something wasn't right. Maybe she was ill, or worried, or grieving her sister. All that blubbering on about the Monroe Miracle pissed him off. He shook his head, catching the frown on the farmer's face as the man white-knuckled the steering wheel along slick snowy roads.

He hadn't said a word all the way to town from Firing Range Road. It was a relief, since Jay didn't feel very communicative this morning. His rig was wrecked and he'd hardly slept. He'd given the old man money for gas. The farmer nodded and started up his beater truck. He continued to chew Bull Durham as he rolled down the driveway that he'd plowed earlier that day. Traveling was slow, as the county roads hadn't been plowed yet.

"Up there," Jay said, "on the left. See the crippled squad car?"

The farmer grumbled. The truck rumbled on. In the sun-heated cab, Jay imagined lying next to Celia, running his hand over a shapely hip and into the deep well of her waist. The scars were gone; he had seen her clear skin with his own eyes. Why couldn't he have just admitted it?

The truck skidded sideways, snapping him to attention. He grabbed the door handle. The farmer slowed a little, steering her carefully back into the icy grooves before rumbling steadily on. Jay leaned forward, squinting against the blinding reflection as he tried to make out what was happening up ahead on the road. There at the turnoff to Celia's driveway, a police rig sat catawampus, its fender pushed up against the mailbox, the post leaning awkwardly toward the barbwire fence.

"Fuckin-A," he breathed. "It's Johnny's cruiser."

Slowing, the farmer pulled onto the shoulder, shifting the truck into park. As he idled, Jay opened the heavy door and jumped out. He turned back to the man, grabbing hold of the door as his feet nearly went out from under him. He steadied himself. "Thanks, Sir," he said. "Careful heading back. It's a skating rink out here."

Jay slammed the truck door and turned toward the cruiser.

Officer America stepped out from the billowing cloud of exhaust. "Hey man, glad to see you. My rig's high-centered," he said, his voice breaking sharply in the icy morning air.

Jay rubbed his gloved hands together, taking in Johnny's creased and whiskered look. "What're you doing here?"

"Sorry, man. Only meant to give your old lady a ride home. Didn't expect goose grease and a blizzard." Johnny wiped his nose on the back of his hand. "Your old lady blew a back tire. As luck had it, I happened along and changed it."

"Bad luck, or good—sometimes is hard to gauge," Jay said, hesitating as he approached. "Whiteout had me overnighting at a farmer's house. Glad the blizzard let up. Now I'm here and my squad car's there. Broken axle."

"Bad luck all around." Squinting, Johnny looked around at his rig. "More snow's heading in, you know." He gestured to the black and white hanging over the ditch. "Got to get her back on the beat. Force is short on rigs."

"We were supposed to rendezvous," Jay said, scratching his chin.

"Sorry, man," Johnny said. "You should have gotten wind of it on the radio."

Jay adjusted his gun belt. The sun's glare off the snow was beginning to irritate him. In the distance, tree limbs cracked beneath the weight of winter. He thought he heard raven wings flapping and turned to look. As he did, he noticed a strand of Celia's curly hair dancing along Johnny's shoulder.

It would have been impossible to see if the sun hadn't backlit Johnny's profile, edging his blues, lighting the springy strand caught in the wool of his jacket shoulder. If it had been anyone else, Jay would have ignored it. He knew how Ceal's hair was; it traveled, picked up here and there on a sleeve, on a shovel handle, on a fence post, landing in his rig, on his living room carpet, and sometimes even in his food. But what he didn't believe this morning is that it got rooted to Johnny's coat innocently.

"Fuck," he exhaled, watching his breath swirl icily between them.

Johnny looked up from his snow shovel where his eyes had remained a little too long. He narrowed them, saying, "Just helping her out, man, that's all. Fucking storm, ya know. Tow's on its way from town."

Jay stepped closer, squatting next to the front bumper to look beneath the cruiser. A winch would raise it back onto the pavement. "You'll need the alignment checked," he said, and stood again, noticing for the first time the little churchhouse; not a curl of smoke rose from the chimney.

Jay nodded and strode off down the driveway. "Goddamned driveway's shoveled. Johnny must have done it. Can't imagine Ceal...."

As he walked the short distance to the house, he worked on calming his fuming irritation, attempting to relax his jaw rigor, just like his therapist had taught him. *Squeeze and relax the fists. Raise and lower the shoulders. Shake out my hands. Rock my head side to side. Breathe!*

"Fuck! Where'd the sonofabitch sleep?"

Star perched on the dresser, waggling her foot as she watched Celia sleep. Snow dripped from the eaves, melting in the bright sunshine, the droplets making a kind of music: *click, ping, drip, click, ping, drip*.

Star thought, *There should be a book of "Celia Directions." Then the poor girl could follow along when lost. Instead, Sissy just flutters her eyes and waggles her hips and some dude reaches out and pinches her ass. Best be unavailable, because she'd make a run for it otherwise.*

Star looked around. Through the walls she could see Jay marching down the snowy driveway toward the house. She stretched her arms toward the ceiling and sailed through the plaster, up between roof joists and outside of the house into the bright sunlit day. She aimed her ectoplasm for Jay's heart, steering him with tiny bursts of energy away from the church-house.

He turned suddenly and slipped around the corner to the orchard-side of the house. "Crap, the woodpile," he said, slipping again and landing on his backside. "I better chop Celia some wood."

Celia attempted to open her eyes, but the glare from the sun streaming through the window was brighter than she could take. Her head pounded like a mortar attack and her stomach felt queasy. She narrowed her lids to tiny slits, letting in a little at a time, the cracks and stains smudging the green ceiling.

Thwack, thwack, thwack.

"Ohhh," she whined, "my head." Then she smiled, realizing that Johnny was out back chopping wood. She hugged herself, knowing that he was helping her with her chores. She caught his scent on the pillowcase and flooded with desire. Stretching luxuriously, she rolled onto her side and jumped as a loud *tap, tap, tap* rattled the bedroom windowpane.

A voice shouted through the glass, "Celia, get out of bed. The preacher's expecting us."

She sat up and squinted into the glare. "JJ?" His face seemed to float, distorted and eerie, through the dirty pane into the room. She grabbed the blankets and pulled them close to her chest. Heart lurching, she turned, half-expecting Johnny to be standing in the bathroom doorway. Disoriented, she turned back. "Be right there," she shouted, and bounded out of bed, pulling on her water-stained silk robe.

Celia dashed across the cold floor into the kitchen. Peering out the front window, she searched the road for Johnny's car. Just beyond the shoveled berm his rig leaned into the ditch, its shiny hood gleaming in the sunlight. Celia crossed her arms over her nervous stomach. "Shit, now what?"

Shivering, she looked around the room for any forgotten pieces of Johnny's clothing. Nothing. Relieved, she rolled up newspaper and stuffed it into the firebox along with several sticks of applewood. She touched a match to the paper and it began to scorch. "Come on, come on," she said, hopping from foot to foot on the cold floor, willing the fire to catch. She knew that any second she'd hear JJ's boots charging up the porch steps, stomping off snow and banging inside.

Popping like hot oil, the wood caught brightly. Celia slammed the woodstove door and ran back to the bedroom, throwing on a red T-shirt, blue jeans, and a pair of wool socks. Out the window she could see Jay chopping wood like a fiend. She brushed her hair and applied lipstick. She slipped the engagement ring back onto her finger and checked her appearance in the mirror. She looked tired, but it would do!

She was the fiend, she guessed; no, not a fiend, a cheater. "Yes, I'm a cheater," she said to the green walls, the bright sun lighting dusty cobwebs looped in the corners. *I'll wipe them down while the sun's still bright*, she thought, and hurried back into the kitchen to grab the broom.

As she walked past the rocker, it brightened. She stopped. Had the damn thing moved? She suddenly felt lightheaded. She stood there, hand to forehead, imagining the walls had begun to swirl. She grabbed hold of the chair, and as she did, the light brightening the rocker faded. The room too lost its illumination. No rocking. No *thwack, thwack, thwack* of wood. She listened, swearing she could hear Star's bell-like voice calling her from the lake. The sound was faint, but real enough to draw her to the window behind the woodstove. She pulled the rocker close to the wall and climbed onto the seat. She opened the window and listened.

"Cheater," the wind seemed to whisper.

"No, I mean yes," Celia said, dropping her head to the sill. "I shouldn't, but I do. I love Johnny."

She breathed in fresh air and the realization of love rushed into her heart. She lifted her head and looked out at the lake, feeling a tenderness for Johnny that she'd never felt for Jay.

As she breathed in the sweet smell of snow, a memory floated over her. She recalled Star rubbing her back in the stuffy darkness of their attic bedroom, the ends of Sissy's hair falling loosely over Celia's bare skin. Celia'd been crying about something and Star had been comforting her. What had happened? She shook her head trying to remember, but a shadow darkened Celia's mind. Like a fading dream she couldn't grab hold of, the blankness numbed her, blotting out the memory. She couldn't swallow. Suddenly, she choked from the pressure of what felt like a sock being stuffed in her mouth.

Celia collapsed, dropping from the rocker to the floor. She lay there, her head hurting where she'd hit the chair as she fell, the cold from the floor soaking into her skin and deeply into her bones. The churchhouse creaked and groaned beneath its load of snow. Celia gasped a breath over the imagined gag.

Thwack, thwack, thwack. Every one of Celia's cells rattled with the sound of Jay's axe hitting cordwood. Then a tiny sleep took her and she dreamed of rodents, pill bugs, carpenter ants, and spiders crawling around her. Once she'd told Raven that her spirit hid between those tight floorboards, amongst the old newspapers stuffed between the joists as insulation, but her friend just scoffed. "More like the Devil, Sugar. He's more 'en happy to wedge ya into a tight place."

Snow melted in puddles around Jay's sodden boots. "Celia?" he said, brushing her hair out of her face. "Ceal, get up!"

She opened her eyes and looked up. "Jumpy."

He thought she said *Johnny* and wrinkled his brow, flinching. "What'd you say?"

"I feel sick, JJ. My stomach is jumpy," she said.

"Oh, I thought you said…." He looked around the room. No sign of Johnny, but that didn't mean he hadn't stayed over. Jay knew people were good at hiding evidence. And lying. "What's wrong with you?"

"I guess I drank too much," she croaked. "The snowbank and that near train wreck, my God, JJ! I could have lost you."

"Huh, weren't you just lecturing me about my drinking? Calling the kettle black?" he said, and took her hand in his, running his thumb over her fingers. The ring looked beautiful on her delicate hand. "You're cold. I'll beef up the fire." He helped her into the rocker, then grabbed the fire poker and opened the stove door. Smoke puffed into the room.

"I need coffee. Will you make me a cup?" she said.

Jay poked at the sparking wood. Groaning, he closed the door and straightened again, turning to the snow-covered wonderland outside. "No thanks. I just want to know what's going on here." He widened his stance. "My new *partner*, Johnny, looks pretty rough this morning. And, so do you. What's the connection, Ceal?"

"There isn't one," Celia said, getting up from the rocker. She removed a bottle of aspirin from the kitchen cupboard and poured herself a glass of water. Her back was to him, small and closed off. Impenetrable. He watched her swallow the pills then busy herself making coffee. When she was finished, she handed him a cup, smiling sweetly.

Jay sipped the nasty brew. "Ceal, I'm a patient man, but I've reached my limit."

"What time is it? Isn't Daddy expecting us?"

Jay looked at his watch. "Eight. What time are we supposed to be there?"

"Nine," she said, grabbing her coat. "We better go."

Jay watched her put on her coat. "What happened to your coat? It's stained."

"Remember, you were going to check my tires? I had a flat. It was pouring rain. I fell in the road while trying to change the tire. Lucky for me, Johnny came along. End of story."

Jay groaned. "Sorry, I meant to. Johnny told me about the blowout."

"Johnny told you?"

"Yes, while waiting for a tow."

Celia fiddled with her scarf, not meeting his eyes as she wrapped the fuzzy thing around her neck. She lifted her black curls to adjust the scarf and Jay caught a glimpse of her beautiful nape. He felt a rush of heat. "Ceal?" he said softly, stepping toward her.

"What?" she said, leaning over to pull on her snow boots. Her coat fell open, showing a bit of cleavage as she bent. He put his hands beneath her coat and eased her toward him. "I want you."

She pulled away, laughing. "Not now! We'll be late."

He released her and stepped back, feeling empty. What did he expect? He had so much ugliness inside of him. He'd killed a man, for fuck sake. It wasn't right, what he'd done to Larry. And it couldn't undo it, ever. "Better button your coat," he said, and stepped past her to open the door. "It's icy cold out there."

Celia walked past him, her hand brushing his as she stepped out onto the porch. "Whatever!"

CHAPTER FOURTEEN

Johnny rubbed his sternum where the thickness had grown into a steady ache. His mother always said he was too big for his britches and now his partner's face would seem to agree with her assessment. But at least he now *knew* what he wanted. And once he *knew* something, nothing could stop him from going after it. That was how he entered the world of policing, weighing his options carefully before taking action. The academy had defined his stature in a public way, shaping his energy to radiate authority. Shame wasn't in his vocabulary. If someone wanted him to feel badly, he shrugged the barbs away. But his keenness also made him aware of the pressure, the internal flinches, tensions that sometimes riled his insides. *E-motions*—that's what the Captain called them. He shook his head. The minute the tow truck freed his rig he would head for that greasy spoon on the outskirts of town. He massaged his chest where the pressure continued to grow. "Hunger—that's it. I haven't eaten since yesterday."

Johnny slipped out early, leaving Celia snoozing away, a tangle of black curls lank on the pillow framing her beautiful sleeping face. He'd decided he loved her. Yes, Jay probably wished him long gone, and the thought had occurred to him—splitting Vinegar Valley—returning to where he'd come from. He tossed another few shovels of snow onto the berm. His stomach growled. Across the field, he could see a curl of smoke rising from the chimney. Celia and Jay stood on the porch.

He was on probation with the Force, which meant he had to stay clean. "Man, oh man," he shook his head. He'd made love to her again and again, despite the spinning she'd complained about. "We should be arrested for joyriding," Johnny muttered, his frozen breath puffing into the icy morning. The clacking of chains interrupted his thoughts. He turned to see the tow truck heading his way.

CHAPTER FIFTEEN

The orchard truck moved steadily down the slippery driveway. "Goddamned mess out here," Jay said. "We're lucky the truck started." But he knew the preacher had kept things in good running condition when he worked the orchard. Even the tires weren't in too bad of shape. And the heavy wood crates the preacher had loaded in the back to move fruit between the orchard and house, gave the truck fairly good traction in the snow. Even then, tension gripped Jay's jaw as the scratchy radio announced blizzard damage: lines down, fallen shed roofs, cars nose-first in drift-ed over ditches, and road closures. Vinegar Valley would be without power for up to two weeks. Rescue stations had been set up for those without heat, complete with blankets, running water, and hot meals. The truck hitched as it pulled onto Route 1, then the engine smoothed out, inching out around the tow truck busy cranking Johnny's rig out of the ditch. Johnny stood back, saluting them as they passed.

Jay drove on. He didn't want to make it into something it wasn't. After all, he wanted to believe his gal was telling the truth. But the harder he tried to relax his jaw, the firmer his teeth clenched. Finally, he reached over and shut off the radio. "The preacher's probably suffering from hypothermia by now. Better set him up at your place."

"No way," Celia said, leaning back against the cold seat, fingers wrapping her steaming coffee mug. "He's probably working on his sermon. You know he'll show up for Sunday service no matter what."

"Keep him for a few days," Jay grumbled. "It'll be good for both of you."

"There're other places he can stay," she said, waving a hand at the radio. "You heard about the shelters: cots, blankets, hot food."

"For God's sake, Celia," Jay said. "He's your father."

"If you like him so much, then he can stay with you at your apartment," she said. "I'm sick of being his whipping girl." She turned to the side window.

"Nice," Jay said, slowing as they approached a nose-first car. He kept his eye on the abandoned vehicle, the truck hitching as they pulled around it. "Nobody there. Must have walked home."

He drove on. "Ask him to pack for a week stay at your place," Jay said. "Don't want another death on your hands, do you?"

"Sheez, JJ," she said. "Why'd you have to say that? You know it wasn't my fault that Star drowned. Besides Daddy's got God on his side. He'll be fine."

"Gad," Jay said under his breath. "You're being a cold-hearted bitch."

Jay shook his head at the cheaply constructed houses lining South Street. They looked like obedient soldiers lined up for morning inspection. "They don't build houses like they used to. Military housing's probably better." He thought of the soldiers out at the base, noting that they'd be recruited to rescue people once the flooding began. Maybe he should leave Vinegar Valley. It took people a long time to get over a big loss. Hearts mend eventually, he guessed. At least that's what he'd been told. Celia and he could make a new start down valley somewhere.

Snow fell from a tall pine at the corner of the preacher's plowed street. As it drifted across the old truck, the sun flashed prisms through the flakes. Berms blocked every driveway. Jay stopped in the middle of the street, midway up the old man's block. He put the orchard truck in park and set the emergency brake. They sat there a minute, neither of them speaking, truck exhaust pouring into the crisp blue air, the fan blowing loudly.

Celia turned and looked at him with kohl-smudged eyes. "What are you waiting for?"

Her look was so full of disdain that he wondered why she was wearing the engagement ring. He sighed. "Go on, get the preacher; I'll shovel the walk while you two duke it out."

"I can't climb over that berm," she said. "Shovel a path, then I'll go get him."

"Fine," Jay said, climbing out. He slammed the rusty door a couple of times to get it to stay closed.

Celia turned, frowning at him through the dirty window. He shrugged and shuffled around to the tailgate. As he pulled out the shovel, Johnny's unshaven face came to mind. *Dead giveaway*, he thought. He'd let Captain Bailey know about Johnny's indiscretion as soon as they finished with storm overtime. "SOB will get thrown off the Force."

The idea of her daddy living in the attic with Star's stuff made Celia feel like she did after the girls all left the club's dressing room in the wee hours of the morning. She had a sinking feeling in her stomach, but then again, she felt woozy from the hangover, so she wasn't sure which was which. It was odd all the same, feeling so creepy about her daddy. She sat in the running truck, holding her throbbing head, feeling the pinch of her predicament. The aspirins hadn't worked their miracle yet. She recalled the dancers clinking together cold brews and blowing smoke rings from their cherry-red lips and her stomach began to roll again. Celia opened the door and swung her feet to the ground. She poured out the dregs of the tepid instant coffee, staining the snow beside the toe of Star's boot spittoon brown. She bent to vomit, but nothing but drool spattered the snowy ground.

Jay shouted from the top of the berm. "Passable now. Go get your dad!"

She looked up, wiping her mouth on her sleeve. "Okay, I'm getting him…," she said, and dug into her purse for a tube of lipstick. She looked in the snow-edged side mirror and pressed *Rascal Red* weakly across her bottom lip, recalling a weirdo at the club slapping her ass, begging to tail her home after the show. Celia had swung around and smacked him hard across the face. He looked so startled that she kissed his cheek, leaving a stamp of lipstick on his whiskered skin. She returned the lipstick to her purse and stood, slamming the truck door hard. Next time she went to the club, she'd be driving her Chevy with its expensive new tires—and once there, she'd toss the preacher's musty church hymnals into the dumpster along with all the stained bar towels and semen-crisped cocktail napkins.

By the time she'd skated around the back of the truck, Jay had a good-sized notch cut in the berm—a nice little path she entered through a cloud of exhaust, high-stepping it across the buried sidewalk and up the path to the front door. She didn't understand why her parents loved this house; it had no character at all, yet it asserted itself against the icy-blue sky like it knew exactly what it was doing. If she were a bird flying over Vinegar Valley, she'd see all the blanketed rooftops, little squares divvying up South Hill where there used to be nothing but fruit orchards. If she were a bird, she wouldn't have such a throbbing headache.

"Don't forget an overnight bag," Jay said.

"Right," she said, remembering what it was like to grow up with an older parent. She'd envied the playfulness other kids had with their parents; instead, her daddy was a stern man in a frumpy sweater telling her to sit up straight and chew her food a hundred times, just because his grandmother made him do the same. She hesitated, preparing herself for her daddy's stern face, feeling the cold on her neck where the scarf hung loose and the coat opened in front, revealing her choice of not-too-sexy clothing.

Knocking, she checked out the steps the preacher had kept cleared. She imagined his snow-removal efficiency to be the same kind of compulsive act as his lectures on Hell and damnation. She turned to Jay, "You're making headway. Daddy will be happy."

Jay grunted and tossed another shovelful of snow from the now lengthening path connecting street to front door. Celia knocked again, imagining Mama turning to the door from where she sat at the kitchen table, reaching for her napkin to stop a drip of coffee from staining the tablecloth. If only it were true that her mama had returned home from the sanitarium.

The house was creaky-cold. The preacher hadn't taken off his winter coat since the power had gone down late the previous day. He'd even worn the old thing to bed. He tried to relax his shoulders, but realized his neck felt warmer with them pressed up around his ears. Outside, chickadees flitted around the back patio, scratching marks in the snow with twig-like talons. He watched, chuckling a little when they jumped and flapped their wings, fighting over golden millet. He almost forgot he was waiting for Celia to come for him, to wrench down hose bibs at the church, drain anything vulnerable to winter cold. He almost forgot that Vanessa was in a state of shock at Luna Sanitarium. He almost forgot that Star no longer walked amongst the living. His favorite child had gone to Jesus. His lovely Star was in Heaven now.

Ed felt the awful prickling starting at the edges of his psyche once again. The feeling used to come frequently, leaving him edgy and dazed. It was the same numbness that had taken him to Hell and back after the funeral. He stepped backwards, the slight rustle of his coat the only thing tethering him to the corporeal world. He'd done nothing wrong. And Hell wasn't for him; no, not for a God-fearing man with an honest heart.

Did he have an honest heart? Not knowing for sure, he shook his head, vowing he'd never give in to the Devil's power, true heart or not. He would write his sermons, preach Sundays, call on his parishioners, and if someone close to him, say old man Higgins for instance, died in his sleep, he'd pray for his safe passage to Heaven while humbly presiding over his service. No, he would never give in to the darkness.

The preacher had stood watching the chickadees for such a long time that he'd begun to shiver. He rubbed his hands together and started pacing again, around and around the creaky-cold living room that smelled of tired Bibles and greasy chicken. On the last pass, his blood moved through his brain more steadily. That's when he spied his Sunday sermon scrawled messily over the yellow legal pad. He needed to finish writing it, but his fingers were too cold to grip a pencil. And his feet, despite the two pairs of wool socks he'd pulled on when he climbed out of bed this morning, were far too frigid to prop atop the recliner's footrest. Yes, even with a throw wrapping his legs, Ed knew he was vulnerable to hypothermia.

So, he continued to pace. Celia was late. The child was *born* late. He remembered the nurse rolling the bassinet into the hospital room and Vanessa, chaste in her pink nightgown, beaming from the wheelchair. Ed had beamed too, resting proud eyes on the pink-cheeked infant swaddled in white, praising the Lord profusely for the wondrous blessing. It was when Vanessa pulled back the receiving blanket to reveal a second baby, all dark and grimacing, that he knew the Devil had dealt him a severe blow.

As the preacher circled the living room, he gnawed on Celia's bad behavior. Soon he was smoldering over the blasphemy of her career. She was a disgrace to the family, working at that damnable topless joint with that scum-of-the-earth proprietor, and then there was that boyfriend of hers, all ego and gunmetal. "God forgive her," he said, fisting his hands just as a sharp knock rattled the door.

The preacher, ready to shout at his daughter, leapt to the door and yanked it open. Speechless, he stepped back. Before his eyes stood his darling Star, smiling sweetly. Her wispy hair framed her wide eyebrows, her smooth forehead crowning the almond-shaped eyes he knew so well. They had that distant look now, as always, a look he couldn't penetrate and at the same time felt invited by. His anger had completely vanished. "Star," he said, stepping forward into winter's glare to embrace her slightness.

"It's Celia, Daddy," she said. "You're flushed. Are you feeling all right?"

"Celia! That's what I meant," he said, and ran a hand through his graying hair, aware again of the lingering dullness that had almost overcome him, a dullness as deadening as frostbite. "Of course, I'm all right."

Celia smiled. "But Daddy, you just called me Star."

"For God's sake, I know who you are." The preacher cleared his throat, sizing her up, his chapped lips and her berry-red mouth puffing icy clouds between them. "What are you doing here?"

"The pipes," she groaned, brushing hair from her eyes with an ungloved hand. "Today's the day to shut off the water at the church, if they're not already frozen, that is. Are you ready? Do you have gloves?"

"Humph!" He shielded his eyes from the glare. "I could ask you the same." He turned to the snowy street where Jay tossed snow like a maniac. He was surprised he hadn't heard the scrape of the shovel or the snow thudding on the growing berm. He hadn't even heard the crunch of snow beneath the truck's tires.

"Pack an overnight bag, Sir," Jay called, leaning on the shovel to catch his breath. "You'll be staying with your daughter until the power's back on."

Ed stepped carefully along the newly shoveled path, moving slowly toward the orchard truck. His own was buried in a huge white mound. He shrugged at the conked-out Ford. If he had to, he'd borrow Etta's car again.

More than anything he wished he didn't have to crawl into the hole today and shut off the water. Celia, all rosy cheeked, flung open the creaky truck door. It wasn't the only thing flung wide. Her coat was hanging open, and beneath it she wore a flimsy T-shirt. The churchhouse had wood heat, and even if it didn't, Ed imagined she'd find a way to keep warm. The tramp!

Cold or no cold, he'd rather stay put. There were extra blankets in the closet and that camp stove they used at the lake would put out enough heat to warm his bedroom while it heated a little soup for dinner.

He turned back to his creaking house. The gray eaves contracted against the weather much like his shoulders hunched toward his ears; somehow the place seemed to be growing smaller as it surrendered to the cold. He too felt as if he were growing smaller—whenever he was around Celia and her boyfriend he felt that way. He stood straighter, realizing that staying with her was out of the question; she was an insult to Christianity and to his authority.

He shook his head. Maybe he'd gotten rid of the camp stove during the move—well then, he could stay in a hotel, or bunk at the sanitarium with Vanessa. It had been a long time since he'd visited his wife, so it made sense to stay there. As he recalled her vacant eyes, a feeling of dread came over him. He could always wander over to Etta's place nearby. He'd probably feel more comfortable there.

"Here, Daddy," Celia said, waving a hand to the truck's bench seat.

"You sit in the middle," he said, and clutched at his chest, feeling the familiar sputter of heartburn that'd been plaguing him lately.

Celia glared at him. The sun was so bright that his daughter's darkly smudged eyes blurred, almost demon-like in their sockets, or was it hatred that she emanated? *Lord in Heaven, free me of this trouble*. But then she sighed deeply and his fear abated.

"Better you sit by JJ, than me," she said. "He's grumpy as an old goat today."

"I thought it was going to be just the two of us." He reached across the distance, tugging the lapels of her coat together, covering her bare neck. "Don't roll your eyes at me," he said, lowering his voice. "There's something I need to talk to you about."

Celia shook off his hands and finished buttoning her coat herself. "What?"

Her glaring eyes seethed. He felt a little afraid knowing his words worked against him when he let them loose. He dug gloved fingers into his palms and forced a smile. "We'll talk later," he said, and climbed in next to Jay.

"Sir," Jay said, "you forgot your overnight bag."

Cringing at the smell of peppermint and stale coffee, Ed leveled the cop with a defiant look. "I'm fine. There's an old camp stove in the basement. We can drop by the hardware store on the way back and pick up some fuel." He removed a flashlight from his pocket and set it on the dashboard.

"Camp stoves are killers, Sir. Your daughter can help you put together an overnight bag, won't you, Ceal?"

"Do I have a choice?" she said, and climbed in, slamming the door hard.

"Maybe you didn't hear me." Ed swallowed, wishing he'd controlled the sharpness in his voice. As he continued, he used the same smile on her boyfriend that he'd used on Celia moments before. "I'll manage; I always do."

"With all due respect, Sir, subzero temps tonight coupled with two feet of new snow will freeze your pipes and you as well." Jay looked at him sideways, his brows lifting as if to say, you know I'm right. "Let's get your things. I'll deal with the taps; won't hurt to let them drip until the thaw comes."

Ed glared at the young hoodlum. "I don't need your help. Now get going."

"Whatever you say, Sir." Jay slipped on his dark glasses and pulled away from the berm. "You know what you're doing."

The preacher listened to the tires crunching the snow-covered street, emphasizing the finality of everything. The truck skidded around the corner, glancing off an icy ridge, careening onto Rita Road.

"Watch it," Ed said, amazed that Jay pulled off a glove and fished inside his jacket for something at the same time he wielded the vehicle down the frozen road.

"Like you, Sir," he said, "I've got things under control." He reached toward him. "Doublemint, Sir?"

The preacher shook his head.

Flicking his eyebrows, Jay looked past him to Celia. "Ceal, you want gum?"

The preacher followed his gaze. His dark daughter removed a stick and folded it into her berry-red mouth. She had dark shadows under her eyes and her skin looked pale. He shook his head.

"Should have done this earlier in the year," Jay said. "Now we'll have to dig out the crawlspace cover."

"I'll wait in the truck."

Jay sighed. "No problem, Sir. Ceal and I got it handled."

The preacher studied Jay's profile. He decided it was the dark glasses that gave him an authoritative edge—his running-the-show mannerism. "Those boys out at the base, now *they're* here to serve. I remember the last big flood to hit Vinegar Valley, the whole platoon dug trenches, dragging caskets out of the creek, saving the town from high water."

"Daddy, JJ's good at what he does," Celia said, patting her father's shoulder. "He protects our community. He helps people."

Ed shrugged off his daughter's hand. He remembered the headlines; Patrolman Johnson kills his partner with a stray bullet. *Some protector!*

The truck turned onto the highway; a spray of snow from a passing plow thudded across the windshield. Jay switched on the wipers, blades thwacking the window edges with a gritty sound that sent shivers down Ed's spine.

Celia leaned forward, head resting in her hands. Ed wished she would redeem herself. Why couldn't she work at the orphanage, or better yet, help the mentally ill at Luna Sanitarium. "The church needs a volunteer to help distribute clothing to unfortunate people. You'd be good at that," he said. "Why not stay after service this Sunday for the planning meeting?"

"I have a paying job, Daddy." Celia rubbed her temples with her fingers. "Remember?" she said, and looked at him sideways, hair falling across one eye.

The look on her face made Ed's skin jump. It had happened so long ago, yet the sound of her skin burning came back to him now. Burning sticks pulled from the fire scorching her young hide. He felt his face flush and looked down, saying a quick prayer beneath his breath. He must rise above this darkness; that was all there was to it.

Sun-glare had him squinting hard. He lowered the visor. A small mirror faced him, reflecting a serene man of the cloth with deeply troubled eyes. He tipped the visor farther down, reflecting his worn winter coat. If his well of loathing were ever exposed to God's light, he'd transform, but would he survive God's wrath in the process?

He looked past Celia, out the side window and the turnoff to Etta's house. Searching the side street, he spied her red sedan buried in a snowbank. She had been at the church on Monday sorting programs and returning hymnals to the pews. While Vanessa slept away at the sanitarium, he'd taken Etta in his arms and kissed her like he'd never kissed a woman before. He shook his head in disgust.

"Daddy?" Celia said.

"Winter," Ed said. Snow rolled away from the chugging orchard truck as it pulled into the church parking lot. The preacher thought, *The snowdrifts look like whitecaps on the lake*. "Breathtaking, isn't it?" he said. "And look at the church—isn't she beautiful?"

"A winter wonderland," Jay said, shifting into neutral and turning off the engine. Thank goodness some of the preacher's steadfast sheep had already been there and shoveled the parking lot. They sat for a few moments, drinking in the sparkling snow.

"The stoplights aren't working. The store on the corner's dark." Celia groaned. "Power's out all over the valley. Staying at the church isn't an option for you, Daddy."

"You'll have to stay at the churchhouse with Ceal."

The preacher closed his eyes against the glare. The two of them were exhausting, always thinking they should decide for him what to do. He had a sermon to give Sunday and hadn't finished writing his thoughts down on forgiveness. "You two go ahead," he said. "I want to sit and rest a few minutes longer."

"Take your time, Sir," Jay said, stepping down from the truck. Celia slid out the passenger side.

"Here's a bundle of rags. You can wrap the hose bibs while I shovel the walks." Jay leaned into the truck. "Preacher, will you be shutting off the water?"

"I always do," he said.

"Okay, Sir." Doors slammed and Celia and Jay continued their conversation outside the truck in muffled tones. The preacher closed his eyes and soaked up the warm sunlight pouring through the windshield. He let his inner vision brighten with Star's imagined smile, her golden hair floating around her serene face like one of those cute angels Vanessa decorated the house with at Christmas. He knew it was nothing more than a trick of reflected light, but still, it was as if she were there in the cab with him.

He rested his head against the seatback, recalling the valley when it ran on wells, when there were no pipes to wrench off in the fall, nothing to heave away at when the first frost came. His breathing deepened and, behind his lids, God's light shone brighter than the snow.

A loud tap on the side window. "Daddy?"

"Be right there," he called.

His dark daughter crunched off through the snow, yet she remained in the shadows of his mind. *Go on Celia, just go*, he thought, shaking his head. On his best days, he'd never think of doing such a thing, but he had black days back then, days when his mores had slipped close to the dark abyss, closer than he'd liked. He recalled her tiny fingers and toes, dips and creases of flesh at her knees and thighs, everything smelling yeasty and sweet. How could he?

His eyes snapped open. He pressed his hand to the place in his chest where heartburn had been troubling him lately. Fumbling for his flashlight, which he'd need in the cellar, he opened the truck door. He walked the sword's edge, all right; walked it with his head hanging low, a despicable Christian to lead his trusting sheep. "God forgive me," he said, and stepped down onto the snowy parking lot.

"Come on Daddy," Celia yelled. "The storm's closing in."

The preacher squinted at the bright sky with the black clouds darkening the horizon and hurried up his steps. Heaving through the knee-deep snow, he headed toward the back of the church. Jay had cleared the crawlspace door and propped it open for him. He was working on the sidewalks now, tossing snow like a madman. Celia was wrapping a hose bib with rags. They'd be done and back home in no time.

The preacher stepped into the crawlspace, hesitating on the top rung, his upper half remaining above ground while his lower half lingered in the darkness. He pulled the flashlight from his pocket and switched it on. The weather forecasters were always blowing things out of proportion. Etta had a decent enough snow car. She'd be in today to fold programs if she could get her car shoveled out, that is. Perhaps he'd wait at the church for her. He thought of the filmy blouse she'd been wearing the last time he saw her.

Right there in the church library he'd reached beneath Etta's skirt and stroked her soft thigh. As he massaged her warm flesh, somewhat clumsily, but apparently adeptly enough, a flush crawled up her neck and she moaned softly; he wiped sweat from his forehead as he took in the blue-black clouds rolling in like Moses leading his flock through the parted sea. "Maybe the forecasters are right," he muttered. Celia yelped. He leaned around the crawlspace door and looked over to where she'd been working; she was on her back flailing in the snow, loops of hose piled on top of her. Shaking his head, he ducked down the narrow ladder, stepping into the dank cellar.

He turned the flashlight toward the shutoff, shining it into the shadows. No doubt a nurse had strategically placed Vanessa in her wheelchair by the tall windows so she could take in the snow-covered forest and gleaming Luna Lake; a beautiful sight even for fixed and staring eyes. He wondered what was going on inside his wife's head today. Cobwebs like the one he brushed aside, he supposed. He doubted she was actually trying to swallow Star's ashes. She was curious, that was all. He prayed that she would once again focus her eyes; perhaps take up where she'd left off, removing her ashy finger from the urn, wiping it off, and preceding with her daily routine despite her grief.

The poor woman was in shock. Everyone at the funeral was. He heard the thud of hoses up top and Celia yelling something to Jay. He ignored the interruption and got himself situated, crouching in the far corner beneath the shutoff valve. All the while he couldn't shake the feeling that if God were a just God, he'd turn back time, give the preacher back Star and his wife.

He used the wire he'd twisted around the pipe the year before to jury-rig the flashlight at eye level, focusing the beam on the main shutoff valve. The area between his shoulder blades stiffened in the chilly air. He zipped his coat up to his neck and hunched forward. He'd done this type of work a hundred times before: replacing hose bibs, fixing well pumps, repairing irrigation systems. Plumbing jobs came with owning an orchard and of course, the churchhouse, which if the negotiations worked in his favor, would no longer be his concern.

The preacher tightened the wrench over the rusty union. Last year, when Luna Sanitarium insisted he care for his wife at home, he'd protested: "Wait, Lord willing, we can work something out." He realized he was betraying his daughter by selling her inheritance, but she'd betrayed him time and time again. What difference did it make? Celia had no say in the matter anyway. *She'll find someplace to live...with that hoodlum, no doubt!*

Groaning, he shifted his position to accommodate his aching calves. The teeth of the wrench clamped onto the fitting. He gave it a heave and the wrench slipped from the valve. "Damn," he muttered, sticking his knuckles into his mouth, tasting the salty sour of his own blood.

He could hear Celia chirping away above. He watched the bright opening, expecting her boots to step down the ladder any moment. She was young and healthy. She'd be fine once the property was sold—in fact, it would be good for her to do something different with her life. Maybe move out of Vinegar Valley—get a real job.

The preacher startled as frozen plastic hoses rattled down the ladder. Snow-covered boots followed. It wasn't natural, all that brightness surrounding her as she descended into the crawlspace; only Christ in Heaven was so brilliant. It was the sun shining into the crawlspace; that was all. He blinked his eyes, adjusting them to the brightness of the opening she'd just come through.

"Daddy, stop swearing," she hissed, stepping into the moldering space, turning toward him as she removed her sunglasses. "The Edens are up top," she whispered. "They brought a big box of coats for the clothing drive."

The preacher adjusted himself into a more comfortable position and replaced the wrench on the valve fitting. "What are they doing out in these conditions?"

"They've got a big rig and like going out in the snow." Celia hauled a coiled hose from the ground onto a large nail protruding from a creosote-soaked beam.

"They're troublemakers," the preacher said. He gave the wrench a wiggle to see if it was clamped securely. "They've complained to the board, you know," he said, stopping to watch her corral the loose coils. "More than once."

"About your swearing?"

"No, about your behavior," he said. "I hate to say it, Celia, but this thing you've got going," he waved his hand up and down to emphasize her figure, "hasn't gone unnoticed. Oh, they're polite enough, but the message comes through loud and clear. You straighten up or I'm out of a job."

Celia grabbed another coil of hose and lifted it onto the nail. "I'm just doing my thing, Daddy. Not hurting anyone. Besides, gentlemen from the congregation visit the club all the time. Did you know that? They're there every week."

"That may well be, but there are such things as God's commandments." He cleared his throat. "Now that we're alone, there's something I need to tell you. This past year the sanitarium's been keeping your mother for next to nothing," he said. "I hate to say this, but Celia, it's because of you that all of this has transpired." The preacher sighed deeply.

"All of what?"

"Well, let's just say, since the accident, I've gone deeply in debt. If I sell the churchhouse, I can cover my bills, with a little leftover to bolster my new church. Attendance is down right now, you know."

Celia stroked her throat. Despite her best effort, her voice broke as she spoke. "You're gonna pull the rug out from under me?" she gasped, her hand reaching for the ladder to steady herself. "The churchhouse belongs to Star and me. You can't take it from us."

"Your sister is dead. The will, the inheritance, everything has changed now. I'm scheduling an appointment with a lawyer as soon as I can shovel my truck out of the berm."

"What about Mama?" she cried. "She won't let you do this to me."

The preacher had stopped listening to his daughter's pleas. He studied the fractured handle, imagining how calmly he'd explained to the cashier that the crack was there when he purchased the wrench.

"Preachers are supposed to be understanding," she cried.

"My decision has nothing to do with you," he snapped. "Now stop your blubbering and finish the job. This hole is getting on my nerves."

"I won't leave my home," she said. "You can't make me."

"I'm in charge of this family," he said. "That's how it works in a Christian family, in case you've forgotten. And God expects obedience." He gave the wrench all his weight and pulled downward. The handle snapped and the raw edge flipped back, slicing his eyebrow open. A streak of darkness flooded his left eye. With his good eye, he saw Celia's terrified expression. He reached his fingers to his eyebrow and felt the flow of blood.

"Daddy, you're hurt!"

The viscous warmth ran between his fingers. Moaning, he dropped back against the wall. Celia was beside him now, her violet scent the same as Star's; the same as Vanessa's; the Monroe women awash in purple violets. Blood streamed down his face as his dark daughter wrapped her scarf around his head, tying it tightly at the back of his skull.

"Hang on, Daddy. I'll get JJ."

CHAPTER SIXTEEN

Celia heard her daddy shouting before she saw the nurse push the wheelchair around the corner into the waiting room. She got up from the plastic chair and stood gaping at her daddy, his head wrapped with gauze and his right eye blackened. Celia felt a surge of protection, and at the same time, she felt angry, hateful even. He was giving her inheritance to the sanitarium. How could he, the old goat?

She thanked the nurse and pushed the chair across the lobby toward the elevator. The preacher grumbled to Celia in a low voice, "If it wasn't for you, none of this would have happened."

"Right," Celia said. "I made the wrench break and fly into your face. It was faulty to begin with, you know that."

"You delayed the church winterization until feet of snow covered the ground."

The elevator door opened and an old man stepped out. "Get out of the way," the preacher yelled, and propelled himself forward, nearly bumping into the man.

"Stop it, Daddy," Celia said. "Sorry, Sir." She backed the chair up and let the man pass. Once inside the elevator, she pushed the lobby button and leaned into the corner, clutching her forehead with her hand. *Too bad if he is old; too bad if his head is stitched and bandaged; too bad if he is a servant of God*, she thought, *I'm through with him. Finished!*

They left the wheelchair at the entrance and stepped outside into blowing snow. Jay waited for them in a loaner cruiser, exhaust billowing into the frigid air. Celia opened the back door and waved her daddy inside. Injured or not, she wasn't going to let him pull rank on her. She wanted to push his head down like Jay did with despicable criminals, but she ignored the impulse and her daddy's protests. Once he was settled in the backseat, she slammed the door, silencing his complaints inside the rig's interior. She climbed in next to Jay, feeling the heat of her anger tightening her jaw until it ached.

"What's this?" the preacher said.

Celia turned. Her father was digging through the duffle bag Jay had stuffed full: robe, slippers, toothbrush, Bible, glasses, and yellow legal pad.

"Who gave you permission to touch my things?" He mumbled something about breaking and entering. "I'll report you to the police."

"He is the police," Celia said, laughing.

"You needed gear, Sir. The blizzard's imminent. I swung by your place after I signed out this replacement rig. Not as good of shape as mine, but the tires are sound. We'll pick up the truck later. It's parked down at the station."

"You had no right. It's my house…my stuff! How dare you!"

"Stop it, Daddy." Celia switched on the radio. Even though it was only early November, Bing Crosby crooned "White Christmas." The preacher sighed, resting his bandaged head on the seat back, eyes closed.

Jay cleared his throat. He was hyper-focused on steering the cruiser through the blowing snow: profile tense, hands white-knuckling the steering wheel, headlights reflecting off the white stuff.

Celia's thoughts turned to Johnny. For as long as she could remember, she daydreamed about *doing it* with each and every cute guy she met. Even while Daddy had her down on her knees praying for forgiveness for her tarnished soul, she was thinking about kissing a cute orchard worker or a sinewy box boy at the health food store.

They'd grown up with a mix of townsfolk and transient workers attending Sunday services in the sanctuary at the back of the churchhouse. Little did Daddy know she wasn't asking for forgiveness with her eyes closed, she was praying for him to leave her soul to her own desires, misguided or not. She hated to admit it, but once she actually prayed for their home to burn to the ground, that way she wouldn't have to be constantly steeped in churchiness. She bit her lip. Now she might have to move out. Where would she go? Maybe she could stay with Raven until she and Jay worked things out.

She caught Jay looking at her out of the corner of his eye. She turned her face to him and smiled. Ever since he'd proposed to her, she'd been treating him like shit. She did love him! Tonight, she'd wear a silk negligee and apologize properly.

Back at home, Celia built a fire. As the kitchen warmed up, she wandered to the window to watch the snowstorm. It was coming down fast, large flakes mounding into knobs and moguls, heaping up on brush and fence posts. Jay stood just beyond the steps tossing firewood onto the porch. Snow coated his dark hair and shoulders. He looked up. She waved. He nodded.

"So, what happens next?" the preacher said.

"I fix dinner, I guess," she said.

"No, I mean, where will I sleep? That hoodlum boyfriend of yours didn't bring my PJs, not even…."

"Daddy, stop calling him a hoodlum. You know he serves the community. The shooting was an accident. Sleep in your underwear, for God's sake. The attic bedroom is above the woodstove. You'll be toasty warm."

"What about…?"

"What now?" she snapped. "We light candles. We haul water from the lake since the well pump is down. We'll have to pour a bucket of water in the back of the toilet to flush it. We'll cook on the woodstove. It's what we've always done, remember?"

"There's a hand pump out by the cemetery," he grumbled. We can haul good water for drinking."

"It no longer works."

"Sure it does. And tomorrow, we'll work on the driveway. I'm surprised you shoveled it. You're not used to hard work."

"Actually, Johnny shoveled it. JJ's rig broke an axle out at the railroad tracks. Johnny brought me home from the service station. I'm having all four tires replaced. They're dry rotted. Very expensive to replace."

"Johnny?"

"JJ's new partner, Johnny America."

The preacher raised his eyebrows. "Better watch himself around you!"

Before Celia could answer, the sound of Jay stomping off his boots interrupted them. The door opened. Red-faced and sweaty, he stepped inside. "Before I head out, I wanted to make sure you've got everything you need."

"We're fine, well, so to speak," Celia said. "You don't have heat either. Why don't you stay here?"

"I have a down sleeping bag good to twenty below and besides, I need to turn on the water, let it drip so the pipes don't freeze. I'll check on you in the morning." He kissed Celia on the cheek and left her standing in the doorway, watching him disappear into the falling snow. She turned and looked at the preacher sitting in the rocker by the woodstove. He was leaning forward, resting his bandaged head in his hands. Her heart swelled for both of them.

CHAPTER SEVENTEEN

The preacher lifted the candle and peered around the attic bedroom. He hadn't been upstairs since Star had died. His chest tightened with what he saw. Even though the candle did little to illuminate the shadowy space, he could see that the room was a mess: plaster chinks dusted surfaces, cobwebs hung in the corners, boxes overflowed with Star's stuff, and the bed where he'd sleep was a wrinkled jumble of bedding.

He set the candle on the nightstand and his duffle bag on the floor. He took a seat on the bed, feeling the grit of ceiling plaster that had fallen onto the quilt when the bombs exploded out at the firing range. "After dinner, Celia can make this right," he said, getting up from the bed to walk to the window and look out at the snowy valley. "The least she can do is give me clean bedding."

From the second floor he could make out the lake, the driveway, the boathouse, and the hills beyond the firing range. Everything glowed blue in the fading light. Fortunately, the weather forecasters had been wrong. He'd seen plenty of Chinooks blow through the valley at night and by morning, not a patch of white was anywhere to be seen. He'd be back sleeping in his own bed by tomorrow.

A clear patch of twilight sky spread across the horizon, reinforcing his belief in his version of the weather report. He puffed out his chest, taking in a deep breath as his eyes adjusted to the low light. He turned to take in the messy attic: his father's and grandfather's boxed up sermons, Vanessa's keepsakes, and Star's belongings were stacked beneath the eaves.

After his babies were born, he felt a degree of happiness. He preached about the purity of God's smile emanating from the tiny beings delivered into his care. That purity was seen in each and every one, although it was frequently replaced with some other force, something darker and more dangerous. The clatter of pans drifted up the stairs from the kitchen. The preacher turned from the window. Take Celia, for instance.... *Yes, she's one of the exceptions*, the preacher thought.

He arranged the flickering candle and his Bible on the nightstand. Celia was upset with him, but the churchhouse was his to do with as he wished. Yes, his great-grandfather had wanted to keep it in the family, but that was eons ago. There wasn't anyone left now to object to what he did. Hopefully Vanessa would wake shortly and return home—only then he might reconsider other possibilities for paying his bill. For now, however....

He wandered back to the window. A final ray of sun broke through the clouds at the horizon and reflected off the lake. The sheen reminded him of all the times he watched his girls swimming, their pubescent bodies dancing around in new bathing suits on the beach. Each year they got excited over shopping for beachwear. Once he stood at the top of the stairs and watched Celia pull on her suit—all that puckering elastic and shiny fabric wrapping her tiny torso. She hadn't cared that he watched her, had she? It was his duty, wasn't it, to make certain she was healthy?

He sneezed. That silty-dust that had drifted down from the trees and mountains, mixing with soot and pollen, had seeped through the cracks around the window and the lath ceiling. Years and years of it. At the hospital earlier today, while he'd sat on the table listening to the doctor ramble on as he slowly stitched his brow together, he actually mentioned the practice bombing and the silt that had fallen from his garage ceiling onto his shiny new Volkswagen. The preacher chuckled into the attic room, although he wasn't laughing as the doctor stitched up his eyebrow. "Goddamned wrench!"

The woodstove door clanked. A whiff of wood smoke wafted up the stairs. The smell of cacciatore made his mouth water. He hadn't eaten since breakfast.

The doctor had only stopped yammering long enough to thread the needle through the preacher's brow. He'd never had many injuries, except for the toe he'd nearly chopped off—but then there was the miracle. *And now, I've been injured near my eye; my evil eye*, he thought.

He'd given *the eye* to Celia more than once and all because he was partial to white; partial to good; partial to purity. He'd seen it in Star from the beginning. He knew he'd lose her someday, because purity always gets lost.

Celia called up the stairs, "Dinner's ready, Daddy!"

"Be right there." He picked up the candle and his Bible from the nightstand, remembering her words from earlier, "Careful on the stairs, Daddy." He took it easy. One step at a time, he felt for the squeaks he'd learned to avoid over the years. He'd been forgiven his trespasses, blessed; yes, blessed and saved, of course. Now his life was dedicated to the Lord. As he stepped into the overheated kitchen, Celia turned to him with the wide eyes of a spooked animal.

The preacher stood at the bottom of the stairs, his moth-eaten sweater hanging askew off hunched shoulders, his Bible clutched in his right hand, a burning candle in his left. Celia stopped what she was doing and stared, stricken by the look the preacher had on his face. Dark eyes peered out from beneath the drooping bandage, his blackened one a terrible fright to see. She was about to speak when a movement caught her eye. She turned. "Alabaster," she said, "get down from the table." The cat jumped down and ran into the bedroom. Celia went back to shoveling scorched leftovers onto two plates. Sighing, the preacher started toward the picnic bench closest to the wood-stove. "Sit on the far side, Daddy. That'll put me closer to the stove, so I can serve another helping if we want it."

The preacher took a seat. He set his Bible next to his plate, and slid his reading glasses on, working the arms beneath the gauze bandage, his fingers shaking lightly. "I thought I smelled something burning," he said, peering at the cacciatore.

"Can't control wood heat, as you know." Celia refilled her wineglass.

The preacher grunted as she took a seat opposite him. "There are ways, if you're careful, to control the heat."

Celia turned to the window and watched the big flakes fall, following a single white one downward. As she stared, she decided as beautiful as the snow was, it also had a violent side to it. She was about to remind the preacher that she knew what she was doing, but when she turned to him, his head was bowed in prayer. It was a pose she'd seen so many times in her life that she was about to join him, but then he looked up; there was a sharpness in his eyes that took her back. Her breath hitched and she brought her hand to her chest. She could step outside; yes, the cold would force her to gasp a full breath. But then a pocket of pitch popped in the stove, startling her. She turned back to her food, picking out a small piece of chicken to chew nervously as she stared out the window. Like a child, she wished hard for the snow to go away along with her daddy.

Frequently, a bad feeling flooded her. When she tried to describe it, she had no words. Maybe she felt like she was drifting away from herself and everyone else. Maybe everybody felt that way at times. She once said to Raven, "Do you ever feel like kicking everything off the shelves at the drug store, then screaming as you run out the door?"

"Whoa, girl," Raven had said. "You're one of them troubled chicks, I think."

Her daddy tapped his fork on the plate. "Your mother's tomato sauce never lets us down."

"I guess you're right." Celia wished an *ah ha* would snap her out of the malaise she'd tumbled into, something to lighten the weight that had her sinking, but nothing came forth to nudge her back to herself. And then she remembered her daddy's eviction notice.

"Daddy, we need to talk," she said, getting to her feet, swaying as she swigged down the remainder of the wine.

The preacher pushed aside his plate. "If you're not going to eat, take the dishes to the sink," he said, flipping Bible pages, squinting in the candlelight as he began to read—*Children, obey your parents in the Lord, for this is right.*

"Daddy, listen to me." A gust of wind blew cold air beneath the door, fluttering the candle flames, dripping wax down the sides of the sticks.

The preacher raised his hand and continued—*Give honor to your father and your mother, as you have been ordered by the Lord your God.*

Celia's head felt fuzzy. Dots of light swirled in her peripheral vision. When her daddy finished reading, he closed the book with a loud flap. Celia jumped, muttering, "Star and I had matching Bibles, remember? You gave them to us."

The preacher didn't answer. As he stared at her, she could see that blood had seeped through the gauze, giving him a wounded soldier look. She lowered her eyes to her plate. Her dinner had grown cold. She picked up the dishes and stumbled to the sink, clattering them into the porcelain tub.

"Careful," he said.

"I am," she said. "That thing you said about giving away the churchhouse...."

The preacher removed his glasses. He tucked the loose end of the bandage behind his ear. "Yes, we'll talk more about that, but first, let's discuss your drinking and carousing."

Celia looked past him. Her boots were waiting by the door. Her coat, though not warm enough, would get her through the woods to the club where she'd find Dan working late. Surely he'd let her sleep in the dressing room. The snow was picking up. There was the boathouse, but the tiny woodstove was probably full of squirrel stores. She would freeze to death out there. She rubbed her sternum, feeling the pressure of held-back tears. There was always Raven's place. It wouldn't take long to get there. Tears flooded her eyes.

"Celia!" her daddy said.

She didn't want him to see her cry. Turning away, she refilled her wineglass, forcing a smile as she turned back to the table. Lifting the glass, she said lightly, "You want some? There's more."

"No, and as long as I'm staying with you, I'll thank you for not drinking."

"This is my...house, Daddy," Celia said. "You can't make me...."

The preacher folded his hands before him. "I'll give you plenty of time to find your own place."

"I'm not leaving my home," Celia said, her voice growing fiercer as she resisted her father. "I'll…I'll get a lawyer. Dan has one. I'll call him in the morning."

"His lawyer's a shyster," he said. "Now, about that bucket. We'll need one to haul snow inside to melt on the woodstove. Only way we'll manage to flush the toilet."

Jay ducked his head, hunching his shoulders against the blizzard. His boots skidded then gripped the deep snow, lurching down the driveway as he made his way to the churchhouse door. Pounding with his gloved fist, he peered through the frosty glass into the kitchen's fractured candlelight, spotting Celia's red-robed blur moving toward the door. He tried the knob. The wind caught the door and banged it open, extinguishing several candles in the cold blast.

"I knew you'd come back," she said, teetering toward him.

In the dimness, Jay thought her hair seemed fuller than usual and her features, well, she looked more beautiful than ever. He grabbed her into a damp hug and rocked her side to side. "Yeah," he said, stepping away. "Wanted to see how you two were getting along without electricity."

"Fine," Celia said.

Her father grumbled from the rocker something about wishing he was sleeping in his own bed, but "no," that hoodlum….

Jay shrugged off his snowy coat. "I know what you mean, Preacher. It's a mother bear out there. I hope I'll make it back home tonight." He hung up his coat and toed-off his boots. Dropping onto the footstool by the fire, he began working on removing his wet socks. He looked over at the old man's bandaged forehead. "You got yourself a real shiner there, Preacher. You're looking a little thug-like as well."

"Friends can often be mistaken for…."

"Stop it, Daddy," Celia said. "I'll get you dry socks, JJ." She hurried from the room.

"Thanks, Ceal." Jay spread his wet socks on the floor next to the fire. Yes, it was common knowledge that he'd shot his partner, but he wasn't sure what to say when people made snide remarks about the accident. Shame could redden his cheeks in a flash, but now he knew they were rosy from the cold, so if a blush had come after the preacher's attack, it wouldn't have given him away. The pressure along his hips from his belt, weapon, bullets, billy, and flashlight made him ache. He got up from the stool and unbuckled the belt. Once the gun belt was safely set aside, he stood warming himself by the fire, feeling the cold slowly dissipate from his ears, nose, even the insides of his mouth tingled in the superheated air.

Celia reappeared with a pair of dry socks.

"These will feel good," he said. "My feet are frozen." He smiled at Celia floating around the room in her robe, relighting candles that had extinguished when the door burst open. He turned to the preacher. "Do you mind, Sir? I'd like a word with Celia alone."

The preacher sighed and picked up his Bible. "What next?" He climbed out of the rocker and with candle in hand, headed for the stairs.

"Daddy and I just finished eating," Celia said, smiling. "You hungry?"

"You're taking your chances with the cacciatore," the preacher said, ducking up the stairs. "It's practically burnt black."

Jay turned to where Celia stood, plate in hand, looking expectant. An empty wine bottle lay next to the pan of leftovers, soiled plates, and napkins. He was hungry, having spent the day shoveling and hauling out ditch-divers, white-knuckling the steering wheel, relocating folks, and writing tickets. He needed to eat. "Thanks, I am hungry."

He felt pulled to Celia and at the same time distant. He couldn't be sure what, if anything had happened between the two of them. Dog shift had left him feeling edgy and suspicious. The memory of his disheveled partner shoveling out the high-centered rig came back to him. *Hardly a fucking superhero. Johnny didn't even make eye contact*. If he showed up in a dark alley, Jay wasn't certain knuckles wouldn't fly. He cracked his own at the thought. He'd find out what went down between the two of them soon enough.

"It's not as bad as it looks—no matter what Daddy says," Celia said, setting the plate of cacciatore before him. "He's in a terrible mood."

Jay took a seat at the picnic table and picked up a fork. "Hurts his ego, staying here with you." He dug into the steaming chicken dish. "Mmmm! Almost as good as the other night," he said, no longer listening to Celia recounting her daddy's foul behavior. Finally, he surfaced from gorging himself and wiped his mouth on the paper napkin. He took a deep breath and turned to Celia. "We need to talk."

"What about?" she said, twisting the diamond around her ring finger. The stone glinted in the candlelight, tossing dots of light across the table.

Jay looked away. "Johnny. What do you think?"

"What about him. Is he okay?" Celia said, and dropped onto the bench beside him.

He studied her sad eyes. Her fingers twisted a curl, a gesture he'd come to know as nervousness. "He's gone," he said, watching for her reaction.

"Gone?" she said, looking puzzled. "Where? What happened?"

"Does it matter? I mean, Goddammit, Celia, he's my partner. Show me some fucking respect."

Celia shrugged. "I don't know what you're talking about," she said. "I mean, you get upset so easily. It hasn't been that long since you lost Larry?"

"Leave Larry out of this."

"Don't yell at me." She looked at him with eyes as black as the corners of the room. The wind howled a steady note, the sound of it reminding Jay of the storm that rolled in the day of Larry's funeral. He imagined he could smell the mortuary, the flaming candles, the officers' wives' perfume, and gunpowder. The wind picked up. A noise at the window had him turning to peer into the darkness. It was just icy snow dinging the panes. Nothing more.

He turned back, took Celia's hand and drew his thumb over the ring. If he and Ceal didn't make it, there were other lakes to sit beside. And rivers, too. Good fly-fishing rivers in other parts of the west. He'd survive, he always did. Sweat bloomed along his upper lip. He cleared his throat. "Where'd he sleep?" he said, pinching her fingers a little too tightly.

"Stop it, JJ! You're hurting me." Celia pulled her hand away. She got up from the table and walked to the woodstove. The firebox door clanked open. Applewood smoke puffed into the air. She shoved in a log. The fire snapped. "He was outside shoveling most of the night. Go ahead, ask him."

The preacher yelled down from the attic bedroom. "Celia, I need clean bedding."

"I better get Daddy's sheets," Celia said. She headed for the bedroom, her robe billowing behind her.

Jay got up and wandered around the room, still looking, he guessed, for evidence. In the flickering light he noticed nothing unusual, not even the empty wine bottle lying next to the soiled dishes seemed out of place. He was righting it when Celia walked out of the bedroom with an armload of bedding. She scurried upstairs without looking his way.

Jay thrummed the counter. The attic floor creaked. Voices filtered down the stairwell in muffled bursts. That night, at Larry's house, his kids were playing upstairs. Jay remembered Laura carrying a basket of dirty laundry down from the kids' room. He'd wanted to comfort her, but when he touched her arm, she threw down the basket, scattering the clothes across the floor. Her screaming fit had him bolting out the door, gasping for breath. He rubbed his forehead, sweaty now from the hot stove, his cheeks reddened once again, this time from the heat.

The ceiling groaned. He touched his socks. Still wet. He dropped onto the stool. Probation wasn't so bad. Yes, a black mark on his record. Yes, he'd have trouble getting another job if he screwed up again. Yes, he planned on keeping it together. He needed a clean record. Life was short; he wasn't going to waste his on an unfaithful woman. No, he'd get a dog. That's what he'd do, get himself a loyal dog.

He heard a soft thud and turned. There was Celia looking prettier than ever, fresh lipstick and newly combed hair, eyes glinting in the candlelight. "Jay," she said. "There's nothing to do out there. Let's go to bed."

Jay rubbed his chin. "We're not through talking."

"Okay, then, why don't we talk about Star's visit," she said. "You believe me now, don't you? I mean, the miracle…you saw it, didn't you, JJ?"

Jay cleared his throat. "What went on between you and Johnny?"

"Nothing," she said, dropping into the rocker. "So if it wasn't Star returning from the dead, then explain my healed skin." She pulled her robe aside and ran her fingers over her slim thighs.

"Ask your daddy," he said, shifting his weight on the stool before her. He grabbed up a fire-warmed boot. "He's the miracle expert."

She opened her legs. "Come on, Jay. Let's go to bed."

Jay pulled on his boots. "It's almost impossible to get around out there. I'll see if the garage can bring your car out from town tomorrow. Until then, you and the preacher will be holed up together." He stood and crossed the room, retrieving his gun belt from the coat hook. As he buckled it on, he said, "Be a week or more, most likely." He shrugged on his coat. "Keep the path to the woodpile shoveled, if you can. Oh, and try to remember what happened. I'm dying to know."

"JJ," she said, running to him. She grabbed his hand off the doorknob. "Don't leave."

"Let go!"

The look in his eye was fierce, frightening. Celia released Jay into the night. Cold wind swirled snow inside, dampening the silk ballooning around her legs. Celia slammed the door.

CHAPTER EIGHTEEN

The preacher always knew when Celia was lying. The giveaway was how she stiffened her shoulders, her eyes looking sideways, irises contracting to pinpoints. Police knew these things too, so *the hoodlum* was probably onto her as well. *In some ways, I'm no better*, he thought, believing he was mirroring God's concern for Celia's soul. So, it made sense to him to stretch the truth to get her out of the churchhouse. He finished making his bed then stepped gingerly down the stairs.

Celia sat flopped in the rocker, chewing on her thumbnail. Already doing poorly and now the preacher had added an additional worry to her life: moving. *She's young*, he thought, *and like all young people, resilient*.

He wandered past her to the window, staring out into the snowy night. "Officer Johnson is out there helping folks, right?" The preacher turned, watching her expression closely, hoping for evidence of what may have gone on between the two young people.

"Guess so," she said, rising from the chair and swaying into the kitchen. "Helping people is more important," she said, "than…," and she raised onto her tiptoes to bang open the cupboard doors above the refrigerator, "taking care of his fiancée." She grabbed down a fresh bottle of wine and twisted off the cap. Glugging rosé into her glass, she steadied her voice as she raised it to her lips, "You need something, Daddy?"

"Aspirin. My head hurts." He shuffled around the kitchen, pinching out candle flames. Circles of soot smudged his fingers. He touched them to his tongue and rubbed them together. "I am nothing but dust and ashes," he muttered, and wiped them on his sweater.

"In the bathroom." Celia stumbled ahead of him, her robe conforming to her shapely figure. She raised the candle higher to illuminate the bathroom. "At the loony bin," she said from inside the small room, "people make payments, right?" The sound of glass breaking. "Dammit," Celia said, "my favorite perfume."

The preacher smelled something sweet, violets he guessed. He recalled Etta's scent that special day in the church library. Suddenly he wanted her like never before. He leaned against the bathroom doorframe, trying for a glimpse of his daughter's backside. "Everything all right in there?"

"It will be once you tell Mama what you're up to, Daddy," Celia said, turning and bumping into him as she stalked out of the bathroom. She stopped, jabbing the aspirin bottle into his hand, "You can make payments, you know."

"Huh," he said, stepping backwards. Her eyes were full of anger, but he wasn't afraid of her rage. In fact, he was suddenly aware of his pelvis. He shifted his weight, his right hip paining him where it had twisted when Jay tugged him out of the dank crawlspace. He touched his forehead, wincing. Blood from his gashed brow had blinded him, spattering red drops across the sunlit snow. His hip would be better by morning, although he wasn't sure about his eye. Would Etta be repelled by him? He studied Celia's flame-lit face. "I've made my decision."

"Watch out for broken glass on the bathroom floor, Daddy," she said, and swung around, staggering down the hall.

He followed her, stopping outside the sanctuary door. He lifted his candle to illuminate the nearly empty room. A long stretch of dark windows lined the musty space. Celia's junk was stacked high atop the altar. And there, in the middle of the floor, a fringed hippie cushion. *Free love's against God's plan*, he thought. He turned to the stack of old hymnals, their shadows dancing like awkward naked figures along the wall. He'd bought the ornate ones with the gilded edges, a splurge for the new church. "You can dispose of those old hymnals," he said. "Or donate them to a fledgling church. That Russian one out on Skeet Road could use them, you know, the one where I donated the old piano." His voice trailed off.

"Whatever," she said.

"But go on doing good and giving to others, because God is well-pleased with such offerings," he said, knowing that giving the churchhouse away was a generous act that would return God's favor. His bill would be paid in full, his church would have a new roof, and a new outpatient building would spring to life on the edge of Lake Monroe; a true Godsend in assisting the mentally ill blend back into the community. "Time to head upstairs," he said.

"Sleep well, if your conscience lets you," Celia said, her voice caustic.

He peered at her shadowy face, her eyes black pools in the candlelight. He said, "You're becoming an alcoholic, you know that, don't you?"

"I'm just fine," she said. "I'm...," she jerked the candle sideways, dripping wax on the floor. "I'm not leaving my home, Daddy. Do you hear me?"

Celia woke in the middle of the night to the sound of the wind whipping snow against the windowpane. She lay there for a while, listening for other sounds until thirst had her throwing off the heavy covers and swinging her feet to the icy floor. On the way to the kitchen, she stopped at the stairwell and listened for her daddy's snores drifting down from the attic bedroom. Knowing her daddy slept just feet away from where she slept made her feel crawly. Satisfied that he wasn't awake, she stepped around the creaking floorboards, moving silently toward the kitchen sink.

Outside, Vinegar Valley was buried in feet of snow. Celia wished Jay had stayed over so they could be snowbound together, curling beneath heavy covers, skin to skin, the smell of their bodies an erotic perfume. The stove popped. Celia jumped. Again, she peered through the shadows at the attic door. In the dim light of the woodstove, she imagined she could see him standing there watching her every move. She squinted hard. Nothing but shadows. She turned back to the sink and drank melted snow from a glass she'd left in the basin. Maybe her period was coming, sometimes the days before she bled, she felt jumpy. Or maybe Daddy was right; she'd been drinking ever since they got home from the hospital. Maybe life was all too much for her to handle.

She ran a hand over her forehead, feeling the bloom of perspiration. Shivering, she hurried back to the woodstove and opened the firebox door. The heat radiating off the burning coals warmed her, settling her nerves somewhat. She took a deep breath and placed several heavy sticks of applewood on top of the glowing embers. She closed the box and waited for the wood to catch.

A tapping sound skittered across the ceiling. Celia looked up. Alabaster stretched and yawned. "Good kitty," she whispered, listening carefully, but all she could hear now was the wood catching and Alabaster's purrs. She closed the cast-iron door and shut down the flue. She walked back to the bedroom.

In the movies, a straight-backed chair wedged beneath the knob kept intruders out. She closed the door and climbed into bed. She wished she had such a chair.

Thinking back, she searched her memory for a reason to feel so frightened of Daddy. There was his constant needling to clean up her act, and as a child, he made her kneel for long periods of time on the wooden floor, praying for forgiveness when she got into trouble. But other than taking away her inheritance, which had her bone pain reeling, there was nothing she could put a finger on that should undo her like she felt undone right now. After all, he was just an old man. She shrugged and pulled the covers over her head. Soon, she was dreaming of the orchard and her fair and beautiful sister.

Celia sprinted ahead of Star, running fast through the orchard. Their Daddy was faster and gaining on the twins, jabbing a glowing stick in the air behind them. The preacher roared something about going to Hell for their sins. Celia looked around, seeking assurance from her sister, but Star was gone. Heart pounding, she expected to see her daddy instead. Nothing but night followed her. Relieved, she slowed, coming to a stop, leaning forward to catch her breath. When she straightened again, the preacher raised the burning stick to strike. Celia gasped awake.

It was barely light out when the preacher sat up in bed, feeling his bladder too full to stay beneath the covers any longer. He dropped his legs over the side of the mattress, touching his slippers with cramped toes, jabbing his feet inside the cold leather. The green sweater pulled on easily enough and as he hobbled stiffly down the stairs, he buttoned one button at a time, crookedly. Flipping the switch at the bottom of the stairs, he found as he suspected that the power was still down. He left the door to the windowless bathroom ajar, hoping for an inkling of light to urinate by. "Celia never brought me the bucket for melting snow," he grumbled. "How will we flush? A multitude of sins," he whispered, putting himself back together as he left the tiny room. He followed the wall to the right of the doorway, trailing his hand over the wainscoting to steady his sleepy gait. Behind the woodstove, he'd once lined up folding chairs on cold winter mornings, each occupied by one of the churchgoers dressed in Sunday's best. Coffee was always brewing in the big percolator, gurgling and sighing and popping as people filed past, shaking his warm hand on their way into the country kitchen. He'd miss the churchhouse once it was sold. For a moment he imagined he smelled coffee and turned to the kitchen, recalling the big percolator sitting on the counter in the corner.

"Coffee, Daddy?" Celia said.

The preacher jumped. There, standing at the kitchen counter spooning instant into ceramic mugs, was his daughter dressed in red silk. He could see clearly out of his right eye, but where the wrench had sliced his left brow, his vision remained blurred. "I didn't see you standing there," he said, pushing the gauze up for a better view of her youthful figure draped in flowing fabric. He cleared his throat. "I need that metal bucket to melt snow for the toilet. You said you'd…."

"Your eye looks terrible." Celia opened the cupboard below the sink. "Does it hurt much?"

"A little." He hobbled over, grabbing the pail Celia handed him. "I'll take care of this. You can fill the iron kettle with snow for hot water."

"I already did," she said, pouring sputtering water into two mugs.

The preacher studied the deep circles beneath her dark eyes, the stain nearly covering the distance from cheekbones to down-turned mouth. Had she been crying? "We never talk," he said, pulling at the hem of his green sweater, realizing it was misbuttoned. He waited for what he supposed would be a confession: *Daddy, Jay left me, because I'm a harlot. I don't know what to do!*

Instead, she said, "I wonder why that is?" She took a step backwards, crossing her arms over her chest.

"We're not close. We've never been," he said, noticing that her posture was Vanessa's when angered; shoulders stiff and rounded. Celia's robe, though tied at her waist, hung open a bit at her breasts. With arms crossed, her cleavage deepened. He looked away, wishing he could just say, *Thank you for taking me in during the power outage. And for fixing coffee.* Perhaps even *bless you*, but instead he let his eyes linger too long. Ashamed, he looked down. *Please Lord, burn this lust from my heart*, he prayed, studying the skim of bubbles swirling across the coffee's dark surface. "Thanks for the coffee," he mumbled, his words hopefully bridging the tangible bitterness between them.

Sighing, she relaxed her arms and reached for her mug. "No big deal," she said, her face expressionless as she turned and walked around him, leaving an exaggerated space between them.

He wanted to say, "What are you so afraid of?" but he didn't. Of course, he'd made her fear him. He'd threatened to take away her inheritance. At last, he said, "I'll melt that snow now. Can't flush without it."

"Knock yourself out." Celia sat at the picnic table, facing the windows. It was growing lighter outside. Snow continued to fall heavily.

The preacher watched her for a few seconds before opening the door to a swirl of flakes. As he stepped outside, he recalled sitting at the yellow picnic table with his parishioners, chatting over coffee. There had been more tables in the kitchen then, three pushed end to end, taking up the entire space between the bank of windows overlooking the lake, forest, hills, and the kitchen counter. For a moment he recalled Etta sitting next to her husband, the controlling and boisterous Robert, who always made his life's accomplishments well known to everyone.

He hunched his back against the storm and dipped the bucket into the white stuff. "Robert, you old galoot, may you rest in peace." The preacher nodded as he smoothed the white stuff off the rim of the pail, remembering his hand finding Etta's fleshy mounds beneath her sheer blouse when her husband wasn't looking. Robert had been gone for more than a year now. He thought of Vanessa comforting Etta and shook his head. He lifted the bucket and stood for a moment, looking out toward the lake. The snow buried everything, shaping the landscape into a lovely white sculpture. It was truly breathtaking. By the time he returned to the kitchen, the preacher was shivering uncontrollably.

"Should have worn your coat, Daddy," Celia said.

"You're right. It's freezing out there," the preacher said. He set the bucket on the woodstove, clunking tin against cast iron, the sound jarring the image of Etta's bare breasts from his mind. He brushed snow off his sweater and moved to the picnic table. Celia stayed facing the window, in awe of the weather or just pissed off, he wasn't sure which. He took a seat opposite her and picked up his coffee mug, wishing she'd turn toward him for a better view of her bare flesh where her robe had fallen open. Absentmindedly, he took a swallow of brew, spitting it back into his cup. He shouted, "You're trying to poison me."

"It's instant!" Celia said. "The power's out, or did you forget?"

Her insolence flared his anger. Soon he'd be asking her for the key to the churchhouse. He turned and looked around the room. "This would put hair on the Devil's chest, as if he needs any," he said, noticing the basement door for the first time since he'd arrived. He remembered Vanessa standing at the stove canning fruit, a mist of sweat bathing her face. "Why don't we open a jar of stewed prunes for breakfast?"

Celia frowned. "The door's locked. I can't find the key. I use the outside door, which I imagine is buried beneath three feet of snow by now. Ask me again in the spring. Actually, you'll have to ask the fucking crazies, since they'll be living here instead of me."

The preacher jerked his arm involuntarily, spilling his coffee down the front of his sweater and pants. "For God's sake, watch your language. It'd kill your mother to hear you speak like that." He blotted the coffee stain with a napkin.

"When was the last time you visited her, Daddy?" Celia waited, her brows furrowed. "Once I get my car back, we'll take a drive up the hill to the sanitarium, then you can tell her yourself that you're stealing my inheritance."

"Your mother needs her rest," the preacher said. "Besides," and the preacher nodded toward the windows, "we won't be getting out of here anytime soon."

Celia leaned across the table, hissing, "If you don't tell her, I will."

"Enough," the preacher said, banging his coffee mug down hard. The remaining coffee jumped from the cup, spattering the table. He got up from the bench, pulled on his boots, grabbed his coat, and stormed out the door.

Snow fell hypnotically. Occasionally, the wind changed directions, streaking flakes across the frosty windows. Celia sat at the picnic table chewing her cuticles. First, she was missing Johnny and now she was missing Jay. And she hated her daddy, the bastard. She listened to the shoveling: *scoop, thump, scoop, thump*. The sound annoyed her as much as his presence did. She was about to run to the door and yell *knock it off*, when it stopped. She peered through the falling snow to see what was happening. There was Daddy, leaning on the shovel handle with his back hunched against the storm. It always happened this way. No matter how mean he was to her, eventually she felt love for him again.

She dropped her head onto her hands and closed her eyes. The nightmare came back to her: a burning stick searing her skin, shards of pain, her sister running next to her and then....

It was only a dream, she thought, lifting her head, watching her father work his way down the path through a swirl of flakes. But then she thought she remembered her mother applying burn salve to her upper thigh and her daddy's hurried explanation—that Celia'd fallen and burnt herself on some coals that had escaped the perimeter of the burn pile.

She got up from the table and walked to the bedroom, the shoveling sounds accompanying her as she removed her robe. She examined her pure white thighs before pulling on a pair of jeans. She wondered if her daddy was right, that prayer was the only true thing; *If so, wouldn't that cancel out Hell?*

"Hell," she said, pulling on a sweater and heading back to the kitchen. She crossed the room to where she'd left her coat and boots. "Nothing to fear when you're already there."

Outside, the air smelled sweet: snow and wood smoke. The rhythmic *scoop, thump, scoop, thump* of her daddy's shovel was muffled and came from farther down the driveway. In the side yard, the snow-laden headstones leaned, some folding like buckled barns to rest against one another. Her stomach tightened as she gathered an armload of applewood that Johnny had left stacked on the porch. She stood there for a few moments, looking out at the vast whiteness, a tightening building inside her belly. She realized suddenly that it wasn't the cemetery that frightened her, but the snow-laden cellar doors. Even as children, when she and Star picked flowers alongside the house to place on the graves, Celia'd given the doors a wide berth. She wondered why the feeling had come over her again.

Back inside, she dropped the wood next to the stove. Her grandmother had canned thimbleberry jam and stewed prunes on the cast-iron stove and stored the gleaming jars on shelves in the cellar. Before the accident, her mother was still canning tomato sauce and soup—but then the water bath boiled on the electric stove not the woodstove. Jay had fetched the last of the dusty Bell jars from the cellar the previous summer. She had taken a swim that day, and upon returning to the house found several jars of tomato sauce lined up along the kitchen counter. That was the first time she'd made chicken cacciatore for him. Even now, recalling Jay's contented eating sounds made her smile.

Celia crouched before the woodstove, waiting for the wood to catch. "I didn't fall on the coals," she said softly, calming her pitching insides as she petted the sleeping cat. "He pushed me!" Sparks spit, puffing out ash as the fire caught. She shut the stove door and got to her feet. Alabaster stretched, yawning. "Wine will settle my nerves," she said, dropping her coat onto the chair as she crossed the room to the cupboard.

Normally, she kept extra bottles above the refrigerator, but today the cupboard was empty. On the counter sat the one she'd retrieved last night. It was half-full. Despite what Jay had said, she'd make a trip to the grocers as soon as Sergeant's Garage delivered her car.

CHAPTER NINTEEN

Peggo's Grill was more crowded than Jay had expected. He took his usual place at the counter and turned up the empty coffee mug. He nudged it toward the moon-faced waitress just as she walked up, setting a plate of eggs smothered in fried onions and roasted peppers before the gentleman beside him. The smell of it made him feel queasy.

"Doesn't look like it appeals to you, Officer JJ."

"You're right, Sweetheart," he said, clearing his throat. "I'll have the usual."

"Got it." She filled his coffee mug and moved down the row, refilling mugs until she reached the end of the counter. Peggo's was running off a generator. Only one grill fired up, but still, hot food on a snowy day when most folks had no electricity; what could be better?

Jay lifted the mug to his lips, breathing in the first savory sip of brew he'd had that morning. His apartment was colder than the preacher's place. *Should have stayed with Ceal,* he thought, looking around. Then I wouldn't be feeling so pent-up. But then again, the preacher was sleeping upstairs.

He adjusted his gun belt and turned to look out the window. Celia's car was in the garage across the street. The parking lot had been plowed, forming a large hill of snow beneath the sign. He'd talk to Tim after breakfast, see how it was coming along. Maybe Tim could deliver Celia's car when it was ready. Maybe later today!

As he swiveled on the counter stool, the leather of his gun belt creaked, and he was back at his apartment looking at gun parts scattered across the dresser. A few weeks after the investigation, the Force had returned his weapon but without the go-ahead to pack again. He'd taken it apart slowly, and cleaned and oiled each piece, and then he'd left the parts sitting on the soft cotton towel atop his dresser for what seemed like forever. Each time he passed by the shiny pieces he couldn't look directly at them. It took him several weeks to get back to reassembling the weapon. Now it was snapped into his leather holster, ready to go.

The waitress dropped off a plain doughnut on a white saucer. Jay set down the cup of coffee and sniffed the air. He liked sweet smelling things: his girl, pastries, and well-oiled leather. He picked up the doughnut and took a bite. Delicious!

He wiped his hand on the napkin, feeling the barrel portion of his gun resting on his thigh, reassuring him somehow that things would be okay, that eventually he'd trust his instincts again. There could never be another mistake like Larry. He adjusted his holster and returned to his breakfast, dipping the last bit of doughnut into the coffee and shoving its sweet sogginess into his mouth.

The waitress refilled his cup and set the pot down. She leaned her elbows on the counter. "How's it going, Officer JJ?"

"Okay," he said, swallowing loudly. Inside he thought *piss poor*, but he relaxed a little, seeing her red lips, so thin and sweet, spreading across her face in a wide smile. "You know how it is," he said. "Wrecked my rig yesterday and my girl hasn't said 'yes' to my proposal yet."

"Maybe another doughnut will make everything okay," she said, winking. "We have chocolate iced."

"No thanks," he said, patting his midriff. "Fact is, I need to get going. On duty in a few." He reached in his pocket and pulled out a handful of change. With it came a square of cardboard. He dropped the pile on the counter, noticing the cardboard was a matchbook from the Toi Toy Club. He covered it with his hand.

She smiled and tipped her head. "Okay, then," she said, straightening up to her five-foot-something height. She filled the roasted-pepper-guy's cup nonchalantly before leaning back toward Jay. "Anything else I can do for you, Officer JJ?"

He studied her eyes for a long moment, thinking how plain they were compared to Celia's. Celia begging him to stay the night had made him feel good, but seeing her hurting like she was, hadn't. He shook his head as he pushed the coins across the counter, the matchbook still pinched against the palm of his hand. "Keep the change."

He shrugged on his coat and ambled to the door. He'd tool past the club on his way out of town; see if that son-of-a-bitch proprietor was working. Celia shouldn't hang around that troublemaker. Yes, he could do it. He could just keep driving, if he decided to, that is; just blow out of town this very afternoon. Leave everything that troubled him behind forever.

CHAPTER TWENTY

The preacher made to-do lists. Now, as he stood at the window watching Celia and the service station attendant talking beside her car, he flipped the corner of a yellow legal pad's pages and began to scribble. Women were always giving him extra work to do. No God-fearing man wanted extra work—well, at least not work requested by *the wife or daughter*. He was the head of the household, after all, as declared by God.

But today he'd made a grocery list like Celia'd requested, hoping to mend the fences he'd broken earlier that morning. He looked over his list: write sermon, chop wood, clear out attic. Did he really need to keep his grandfather's old sermons, or could they go to the dump along with Star's belongings? He'd have to do something with all those boxes stored in the attic once Luna Sanitarium took over the church-house. He smiled a little to himself, feeling good about his decision to pay off his debt to the sanitarium.

The Sergeant's Garage attendant handed Celia an envelope that the preacher assumed contained an invoice. A curl of exhaust drifted off toward the lake from Celia's defrosting car. He watched the plume drift past pointed caps of snow-topped tules and recalled his grandfather receiving the Monroe Miracle after drowning in the lake. Yes, there were confirmations of miracles found in the Bible. Generally, they had to do with Jesus or saints, not ordinary people like the Monroes.

It made sense to him that the congregation didn't like hearing about such phenomena. He guessed they were reminded of charlatans and snake oil salesmen. Maybe even the Devil. He took a seat at the picnic table and tapped the pencil on the legal pad. "The Monroes have had a long history of miracles," he said to the cat.

The Devil likes fooling the living, making folks think a miracle is from God, he thought. Once the preacher had actually seen the Devil play out his trickery right in the backyard cemetery. Yes, the apple tree he'd planted bloomed midwinter. It wasn't an exotic fruit tree—just a new variety of apple he'd wanted to try, something that would keep longer than the fruit the old trees were producing.

It was the winter before Star's accident. As usual, he'd left the churchhouse early one morning for his daily walk around the lake. And when he returned, there it was, the tiny tree abloom in pink flowers, the blossom's lushness radiating the purest light he'd ever seen. He stepped across the frosty grass, winding his way between the headstones to check out the phenomenon. All at once, Jesus appeared just beyond the blooming tree.

He'd dropped to his knees. "Lord, what is it?"

The Lord's arms reached wide, His heart emanating a light so pure that the preacher remembered bowing his head and weeping.

The fire popped and the preacher nearly jumped off the picnic bench. He looked around the room, shivering as he recalled the sound of the kitchen door banging open that day. Vanessa had cried out, the panic in her voice switched the following events to slow-motion. He'd gotten to his feet, turning from the beautiful tree to watch his wife running across the yard. "The Miller's boy…he's killed himself," she cried.

When he'd turned back to the cemetery, the tree was brittle, as one would expect on a frozen winter's day. Yet strangely, there on a gravestone lay a pile of ash, like burnt newspaper, the sole remains of the Lord's appearance. When he reached out to touch the Lord's ash, it shifted, like a leaf scuttling on a breeze. When he actually touched his finger to it, a flash of great darkness rushed through him. He fell backwards. Vanessa screamed.

Scratching his wrapped head, he turned back to the window and watched the tow truck drive off, its red taillights a blur in the whiteness. He shook his head. That was all he remembered from that day, except for the sermon he wrote detailing the tricks the Devil will play. "He'll play them on any one of us, even Jesus," he muttered, watching Celia walk through the snow toward the house. "We must be very careful."

He crossed out the topic *Compassion* and wrote *Trust* instead. Here was a topic he could sink his teeth into. He set down his pencil and picked up the mug of now-tepid instant. He wished he could call Vanessa in from the other room, ask her to bring him a warm cup, but no, she was asleep, so to speak, up on that icy hill at the godawful sanitarium. He rubbed his bandaged forehead, suddenly feeling fatigued. Even though he visited Etta occasionally, he hadn't seen her often enough to keep a man satisfied; even God-fearing men have needs.

The door banged open and Celia swooped in on a swirl of snow. "Get ready, Daddy. We're going to the store."

"What if we get stranded in a blizzard," her daddy said, tossing the shovel into the trunk of the Chevy.

Celia shrugged, not knowing whether she would make it to town and back. Her car was heavy enough and with the new tires, they'd be steady on the road. She climbed in, moving the grease-smudged envelope off the dashboard to the glove compartment. She'd worry about paying for the tires later.

The preacher climbed in next to her, shouting over the blowing heater about a certain type of cracker he wanted to pick up. She thought he was saying Respect, but there wasn't a cracker called Respect that she knew about. She put the car in reverse and backed it around. The tires had real holding power. She turned the wheel and headed down the driveway without a lick of slipping. She guessed they were worth whatever they cost.

As she drove, the preacher mused over his grocery list, muttering peanut butter, bread, milk. Celia accelerated, testing the new tires on the plowed road by slamming on her brakes. She fishtailed, turning the wheel into the spin until the tires grabbed and they rolled on steadily.

"Careful," the preacher said, pushing at the gauze that sagged over his injured eyebrow.

"I am."

He went back to his grocery list. “We can keep food on the porch; it’s cold enough. And I’ll do some of the cooking to give you a break. Your mother and I used to cook on the woodstove, you know.”

Celia nodded, barely listening to the preacher’s story about her mother cooking bacon and eggs. Johnny had a little apartment in town, across from a convenience store. Maybe she could visit him while her daddy did the shopping.

“Raisins,” he burst out. “That’s what I want on my breakfast cereal, and bananas, too.”

“Okay,” she said, turning onto the highway and accelerating, heading north toward the club. Hill Road was considered a shortcut. The roads were plowed, but hardly anyone was out. Probably a good thing, since the snow was falling hard enough again to turn things dicey soon.

“Canned soup,” she said, wondering why she hadn’t insisted on leaving him home. “And a jug of wine.”

“What did I tell you?” the preacher said, his voice raised over the blowing heater. “You drink too much.”

Celia frowned at her daddy but didn’t respond. She knew she was a good daughter, despite what her daddy thought of her. And no matter what, he was never pleased. How long could she put up with taking care of him? She tapped the brakes, slowing to the stop sign. For a moment, she thought of Johnny in her bed, a candle lit on the nightstand, the scent of him as he reached his soft hands to encircle her. A longing grew in her heart that felt almost unbearable. She decided that while her daddy did the shopping, she would run across the street to Johnny’s apartment. And even though there were no other cars on the road, she put on her blinker and turned left onto Golden Road.

“Why are you going this way? The supermarket uptown is better,” the preacher said. “They have the crackers I like.”

“This is closer. I don’t want to be gone long. See how the snow’s mounting up again?” Celia gripped the steering wheel more tightly. The windshield wipers thwacked, forming a ridge of snow along either edge of the window. The defroster blew clear circles in the middle of the condensation. “We’re not far from the turnoff to Luna Sanitarium. We could pop up there and explain to Mama your plan to kick me out of my home. Maybe that'd wake her up."

"Silence, Daughter. As head of household, I'm in charge of my family."

"You and Mama. But not me? Jay asked for my hand, you know."

"I saw the ring the hoodlum gave you," her father said, and went back to his legal pad, continuing to write his list. "Oh, for Heaven's sake, stop sighing like that."

"I'm not sighing."

"I heard you, Celia. You like making me out to be the bad guy, don't you? Again, I'm just looking out for your own good and your mother's, too."

"It's not that. I'm nervous about the roads."

"Do you have mayonnaise?"

"If Jay didn't eat it all."

"Does he eat at your place every night?" The preacher leaned toward her. "It isn't proper, you know."

Celia laughed. "We're engaged now."

"Why a cop would fall for…."

"Daddy, stop it." Celia pulled up in front of the grocery and shut off the engine. "I've taken you into my home so you don't freeze to death. Be nice to me."

"Humph!"

The two of them sat there for a few moments watching the snow silently blanket the windshield. She opened the door to the hum of the store's generator and climbed out. "Go ahead and shop and when you're finished, wait inside the store. I have an errand to run. I won't be long."

"Where are you going?" he said.

She closed the door, shutting out his muffled cry, "Celia!" When she reached the other side of the slippery street, she turned back, watching her daddy disappear into the store. That's when she realized he'd been saying Ry-Krisp all along.

Celia opened a door into the musty entryway of an old apartment building. Maybe it was a mistake to visit Johnny, she didn't know for sure, but she wanted him and that was all she could think about. She almost felt giddy turning to the row of tarnished brass mailboxes, some with clothespins clipped to their covers. Number 201 had Johnny's name penciled onto a smudged bit of paper folded into the name slot. She buzzed the bell and waited. No answer. She looked around at the tiny space—the rickety railing, the narrow hall heading to apartment 101 in the back—and felt incredibly lonely. She missed Star. She missed Mama. She was alone with her problems, sinking deeper into the dark abyss. Where was Johnny?

She reached to touch the buzzer again when the door creaked open behind her. Turning, she watched Johnny step in from the street. His cheeks were rosy. The shoulders of his blue peacoat were covered with snow, as was his stocking cap.

"Celia. I didn't expect...."

"Johnny." She grabbed hold of him, hanging on tightly, tears welling in her eyes.

"Hold on," he said, pulling away. He drew his gloved finger across her cheek. "You must be freezing in that light jacket. I've got a blanket upstairs. Come on."

"Daddy's buying groceries. I only have a few minutes."

Johnny waved her ahead of him. As she passed, she smelled car exhaust and the faint scent of cinnamon. They climbed the creaky stairs to the first room on the left, where he stepped around her and unlocked the door.

"You should have stayed home," he said, opening the door into his spare apartment. "The roads are dangerous. Black ice. Wind. And more snow coming in."

"I'm okay. You know, expensive new tires," she said. She looked around the room. Only a few pieces of furniture and no curtains on the windows. Cold radiators, a twin bed neatly made, an extra blanket folded at the foot. Washed dishes stacked in a sink drainer. She looked down. Her snowy boots were making puddles on the linoleum. "Sorry."

"No problem." Johnny removed a newspaper from a chair and offered her a seat facing the window. She thanked him and sat down. Outside, snow fell steadily. The light was fading. Her visit couldn't last long as the roads would turn treacherous soon.

"What's going on?" Johnny said, wrapping a blanket around her shoulders.

"I thought we could…you know, see each other still."

"I'm not so sure about that. I mean…."

Celia remembered the dream that had been plaguing her all day. She was running through the orchard just ahead of her daddy. Shivering, she pushed the dream away and focused on Johnny's concerned face. "Daddy's staying with me while the power's out." Celia picked at the fingernail she'd chewed off earlier. "He's mad about the weather. Everyone's mad."

Johnny pulled up a chair and sat facing her. He removed his gloves and took her hands in his. His eyes were dark shadows in the low light. He smiled. "I'm not."

Suddenly she felt shy. Behind him, ice crept along the windowpanes. She wanted to get up from the chair and walk to the window, look across the street to see if her daddy was waiting for her. Instead she said, "Raven reads divination cards. I think…well, I know she said that there was something about us being, you know, together." Her tongue found her top lip for a moment as she lowered her eyes. When she looked up again, Johnny was leaning in to kiss her.

It was a slow kiss that jumbled her insides even more than they already were. When he released her bottom lip, she turned to the window, lifting a hand to her mouth.

"Celia?"

She turned back, smiling shyly. "It's okay. I want to stay longer, but Daddy…I just have to check." She got up from her chair and walked to the window. Across the street she caught a glimpse of the preacher waiting at the checkout counter inside the little store. "I gotta go. He's checking out."

"Celia," Johnny stood, rolling his hands together. He looked around the room. "They're giving Jay someone new."

The generator hummed, flickering the lights in the corner grocery. The preacher rubbed his eyes. His nose was cold. His feet too. Across the counter, the pimply-faced checker wore a Santa hat. The preacher sighed, watching her bag bananas, cornflakes, milk, tomato soup, bread and peanut butter. She dropped the box of Ry-Krisp he'd found atop the cracker shelf into the bag. Salivating, he looked down at his hands.

In front of him, on the counter sat a box of matchbooks. They needed matches and utility candles to get through the power outage. He was reaching for a book when he saw the advertisement for the strip club where Celia danced, and flushed with rage. He almost scooted the matches off the counter into the trash while the clerk wasn't looking. Instead, he drew his hand back, checked the store for other customers, and imagined his beautiful wife, the way she sat so still these days at the sanitarium, like Lot's salt family. He wagged his bandaged head. He would go for a visit soon.

"You buying those matches, Sir?"

"What?" he said, scratching the stitches beneath the gauze.

The cashier nodded toward the preacher's hand, which still hovered near the box of matchbooks.

"Oh, sure," he said and removed a book from the box, bending the cover between his thumb and index finger to conceal it. "Please," he said, tossing it into the bag.

Beyond the checker, out the window, he could see Celia step out the door of a dilapidated apartment building across the street. She turned and waved to a shadowy figure hovering in the second-floor window, then slipped across the street toward the store, hands in her coat pockets, snow dusting her black curly hair. *Where's her hat?*

She turned to look at her car and he saw her fairness, her red lips and pink cheeks. *She's innocent, really. Perhaps my move to give the churchhouse to the hospital is a bad idea; after all, she isn't evil, just flawed—like most people*. He cleared his throat, shaking his head again. "Does she remember what happened? Of course not."

"Sir?" the checkout girl said.

"Oh, add in three more books of matches," he said, "and two packs of those utility candles. Big storm's coming, and my daughter," he said, pulling a wad of bills from the money clip, "I'm staying with her. Here she comes now."

Celia walked inside. "I thought you'd be done by now," she said, stepping up beside him.

"Almost." He smelled the damp wool of her coat and her violet perfume. He grinned, turning back to the clerk. "You look like a good Christian girl. We need some help at the church. Come by for an interview. Maybe you can head up the clothing drive." He reached out his hand to shake hers.

Celia groaned.

"What, you don't want the job. She might."

"I'll be in the wine aisle," she said, and hurried off.

Snow fell steadily, sparkling in the headlights. In the back seat, several bags of groceries rustled around. The preacher sat hunched beside her, the fabric of his coat swishing as he turned and pointed, directing Celia to slow, to be careful, to watch out for ice, to, to, to....

I know what I'm doing," she said, feeling the sharp edge of her longing for Johnny distracting her attention. She imagined the kiss again and slowed the car to a crawl, turning into the driveway. The lake was barely visible in the snowy dusk. She drove slowly down the driveway, parked and turned off the engine. The two of them carried groceries inside and when her daddy left to haul wood from around back, Celia put the groceries away.

Celia barely spoke to her father the entire drive home. Now she walked around the kitchen lighting candles, stopping at the window, watching Daddy shuffling around the corner of the churchhouse, a load of wood in his arms, hat pulled down over the gauze wrapping. His comment to a total stranger about working at the church had raised her hackles. Yet, in some weird way, he seemed proud of her. The preacher dropped the wood on the porch with a loud thud and dusted off his hands. He opened the door and stepped inside.

"Daddy, I need to talk to you about something."

"We've already been over this," he said, removing his snow-covered hat. He adjusted his bandage. "Now, I'm hungry. Sandwiches for dinner, okay? We'll have some tea, too."

Celia poured herself a glass of wine and took a seat at the picnic table. "Not about that," she said, "about a dream I had last night."

He turned his back to her and slowly removed his coat. He hung the sodden garment over a hook next to the door and pulled off his boots. He pulled out his handkerchief and blew his nose. He cleared his throat, "Dreams mean nothing," he said curtly. "They're just the brain sorting information. Everyone knows that."

"Daddy, about my burn scars. I don't think I fell on the pile of coals like you said I did. I think you poked me with a burning stick."

The preacher hesitated, eyes lowered, pushing at the gauze like wrinkled skin. "There were always fires to tend between the orchard rows," he said. "I've been burnt many times. You fell, all right." He pushed up his right sweater sleeve.

Celia's breathing quickened. The gesture happened before whippings; she figured most kids got beaten when they disobeyed. She tightened her sweater around her torso and leaned closer to her wineglass. "I don't think...."

"See," he said, pointing to a white crescent shape stretched across the inside of his forearm.

"I have something to show you too," she said, getting up from the table. "I'll be right back."

In the chilly bedroom, Celia stripped off her jeans and sweater and pulled on her robe. She returned to the dimly lit kitchen, approaching her father who stood at the counter removing slices of white bread from the newly purchased loaf. "Look," she said, pulling aside the silk.

"For Heaven's sake," he said, and looked away. "You're not decent. Cover yourself."

"Daddy, look at my thighs." Shyly, she parted the robe, revealing the new skin where there'd once been angry red scars. School kids always asked her about it at summer lake parties. They'd point and say, *What happened there?* She'd reply vaguely about an accident in the orchard. How she and Star were running, how she'd tripped and fell in a burning pile of coals. Everyone repeated the story.

"There's nothing to see," he said. "Besides, the light's getting bad. Now, sit down. I'll make you a sandwich."

"Listen to me, Daddy. Mama put ointment on the blisters, right here in the kitchen. I remember you lifting me onto the counter, then standing over there, by the basement door." Celia turned, recalling the scene in her head. "You explained to Mama how Star and I were chasing each other and how I'd tripped and fell in the coals. But really, it was you—you were chasing me, Daddy. But why?"

Celia could hear the fright in her own voice. "Why would you do a thing like that, burn your child with a flaming stick?" She stood now, fisting her hands. "Why would you knowingly harm me?"

"Things get confused with time," he said, slathering peanut butter onto the bread. "You're making all this up. Nothing like that ever happened. And look, not a blemish on your skin—that proves it, right? End of story."

"I have proof," she said, bolting from the room a second time. Celia rummaged through dresser drawers until her fingers found the edge of a photo she'd hidden beneath her folded underwear. She and Star posed on beach towels that summer, wearing new swimsuits, both smiling sweetly. And there they were, angry red burns marring the top of her thighs.

"I've made up my mind," the preacher said when she reentered the room. He was sitting at the table now, a sandwich, glass of milk, and Bible before him; across from him he'd set a plate with a sandwich cut in quarters next to Celia's wineglass. "Accidents happen. Nothing will change that," he said, and slipped on his half-moon glasses. He flipped through the Bible, its worn pages opening to a favorite Psalm. "Now drop it, please."

"Look," she said, tossing the photo onto the open book.

He shook his head, pushing it away with shaky fingers. "See what the Devil's elixir has done to you. Alcoholics become delusional with time, Daughter."

"I'm not an alcoholic," she said. "You're kicking me out of my home; at least have the decency to listen to me. You did this." She pushed the photo closer to her father and snapped, "Look at it!"

The preacher squinted at the image and handed it back to Celia. "It could be jelly for all I know."

"The other night, Daddy, I saw Star in the woods," Celia said. "She came in a vision, asking me to remember something that happened when we were little. And now I have. It was Star who healed my burn scars, Jay will tell you so. He was here when the Monroe Miracle happened."

The preacher flipped through the Bible. He cleared his throat. "Let's pray, Celia."

"Daddy, you can ask him yourself. He'll tell you about me falling in the shale. It was Star who gave me the miracle. Look again. The scars, they're completely gone."

The preacher looked over his glasses. "It's always something with you, isn't it? Maybe it can't be helped, this rebellious streak of yours. After all, being a preacher's daughter demands proper behavior that doesn't come natural to youth. The pressure you were under—and obviously still are—is difficult at best. But somehow, your sister managed to be a good person. Let that be a lesson to you." He shook his head. "Now, let's pray."

Celia curled her hands into fists. "Ohhh! I hate you," she said, whirling about. She grabbed her coat from the hook, slipped on her boots, and slammed out of the churchhouse into the blowing snow.

The preacher stood at the kitchen window, his fingers white-knuckling the windowsill as he squinted through the storm trying to see where his daughter had gone. He watched for the red of Celia's robe flying below the hem of her wool coat, realizing it would soon be too dark to keep sight of her. The wind gusted, streaking snow across the yard, blotting his view entirely. "Star," he whispered. "Bless your soul in Heaven. Please take care of your sister."

The preacher knew that miracles healed the Monroes after accidents, not small accidents like a bump on the head as he'd experienced in the crawlspace, but large ones, like when he'd nearly chopped off his toe splitting wood. And his amazing grandfather who had drowned and when pulled from the lake, sat straight up, spouting lake water and laughing heartily. Yes, his grandfather had shaken hands with Jesus and come back to spread the good word to anyone who would listen. Seems there was no stopping a Monroe.

Except for Star. God failed to revive his golden daughter. His hands drew back from the cold sill, fisting with grief, rough nails digging into his palms. One of Star's shoes had sat on the beach for the rest of that week. He peered through the snowy glass, his eyes filling with tears. Even after they'd hauled her to the morgue, that blasted shoe sat there on the beach.

He dried his eyes with his handkerchief. A woman had never been granted the Monroe Miracle, and if one had been bestowed on a female, it would have been Star, not her harlot sister.

He shook his head as he peered through the frosty pane, glimpsing his dark daughter leaning into the blowing snow, the red of her silk robe like a bloodstain against the winter white. If Celia wasn't lying, then it was Star he'd seen standing on the porch the day they'd turned off the water.

He grabbed his chest, feeling the tightness that came and went, indigestion he guessed. He'd take an Alka-Seltzer before bed. Emotional bitterness was stuck in his throat, pinching it closed; he dropped his head into his hands in disgust.

"Oh, Vanessa, what have I done to our family?" He yearned for the feel of his wife's cool hand on his forehead. Forgetting his bandage, he rubbed his forehead, groaning at the roughness of his palm snagging the stitches in his eyebrow. Yes, he remembered dragging Celia down from the apple tree, chasing her and striking her with a burning stick. Was it Easter or Palm Sunday, or had the season changed to summer; was camas withering on the lake shore? "Oh, God forgive me," he said, and despite himself, he began to weep.

The preacher wiped his eyes with his handkerchief, stuffed it back in his sweater pocket and turned to the window, peering through the frosted glass. He saw nothing but twilight and falling snow. He pulled at the gauze, looking harder, resisting the memory of slapping Celia to the ground when she was a tiny child. Yes, after Star's death he'd taken the axe and chopped the canoe to pieces, doused it in gasoline, and tossed on a match.

Anyone could forgive the actions of a grieving father who'd temporarily lost his mind. He flinched at the hiss of wood in the woodstove, recalling the searing sound of Celia's delicate skin. He would have burned her again, if he'd had the chance. "God forgive me!" he cried, bringing a rough cuticle to his teeth and biting down hard, just as the door opened and in blew his daughter, shivering beneath her snowy shroud.

"Why'd you run off like that? I was worried sick," he said, helping her off with her coat. "You're soaked; you'll catch your death."

Celia pressed blue fingers firmly against her quivering lips. Her eyes were wide and red with tears and cold. The preacher helped her into the rocker, wrapped her in a wool blanket, like he did when he sat with a parishioner waiting for a confession. The stove popped, releasing a puff of apple smoke into the room. He heard the ticking above, a sound coming from the attic. Shivering, he looked up just as Celia burst into tears. He returned his focus to her. "There, there," he said.

Celia wept. "She's gone, Daddy, gone. It's not my fault. We were in the canoe. I…I didn't believe what she'd said about you and we argued. She jumped up, angry with me, insisting I remember what happened when I was little."

The preacher pulled the handkerchief from his pocket and handed it to her. Celia pushed it away and blubbered on. "She was shouting and swinging her arms. And then the firing range…a loud explosion. She lost her balance, hitting her head on the oarlock when she fell."

Celia dried her eyes with the sleeve of her robe. "I…I tried to save her," she said, shaking her head. "I went after her into the lake. She was all the way to the bottom, Daddy. I still can't get the look on her face out of my mind." Celia looked up at the preacher, her eyes wet and dark and piercing. "I remember now," Celia said. "You burnt me with a stick, more than once. But worse than that, Daddy, you raped me."

Stunned, the preacher shook his head. "No!" he said, "No! That never happened." He dropped onto the stool, clutching his gauze-wrapped head, wrestling against the darkness that threatened to pull him under, the Devil curling a finger at Edward Monroe. *Come with me, it's time to go.*

Celia sat before him like a beaten animal, her shoulders sagging, her hands clutching her throat. If he chose the right words and spoke them in a kind manner, everything would return to normal. "Why don't you lie down? I'll help you to your bedroom." He took her arm and pulled her to her feet. "You're feverish, talking nonsense. Sleep will make everything better."

Celia's eyes blazed. "I'm not sick, Daddy." She jerked her arm free, flying at him, hands flailing his chest. He stumbled backwards. "You won't get away with this, old man."

"Stop," he said, catching himself against the kitchen counter. He raised his arms to protect his face from further attack. Instead, Celia turned and ran from the kitchen, disappearing into the bedroom, the door slamming loudly behind her. The ticking sound flicked across the ceiling following after.

CHAPTER TWENTY-ONE

Star clung to the curled edge of a giant lily pad, riding out the storm on its surging mass. Her hair had tangled together with lake weed, lank strands catching snow in twists as the wind whipped around her. Finally, tired of sloshing about, she slipped beneath the water, becoming the lake with its current and fish and black tangled lily roots.

From the billowing silt below, Star watched snow spattering the surface above. Unlike Daddy, she knew there was no death, just the freeing of spirit from the body once physical life ceased. Her daddy always said death would put her under the ground until the Rapture when the chosen were lifted up to Heaven and welcomed into the Lord's arms. But really, the Rapture was nothing more than life without a body. Couldn't he see that?

It was wondrous being a spirit. Star smiled to herself, then frowned as she recalled her sister running through the blowing snow across the yard to the lake. Celia sought to free herself of her burden. Maybe sleeping with random men would no longer be her Heaven. From where Star rested on the stormy lake bottom, she'd watched Celia fly at Daddy, fists flailing. Maybe she'd be able to move on now that the secret was out. Then, Star could move on too.

Star tried on her sister's flailing gesture, wishing she could pummel the preacher as well, but for now, the water rushed her, spinning her upward, flinging her about on gusts of chortling wind, across the snow-covered yard to the steps of the little churchhouse.

She slipped through the wall like water through fingers, floating past her daddy who stood dazed in the candlelight, leaning over the woodstove, scratching his bandaged forehead. She knew he felt despicably miserable and was glad. She'd deal with him later.

Star floated into the bedroom, ticking across the ceiling on her way. Her bluish glow hovered above Celia. She looked so tiny curled beneath the blankets, her knees pulled against her heaving chest. Star slipped beneath the covers, forming her cells into a spoon-like shape, pressing them against her shivering sister. She remembered the burning ache of chilled hands when warmed too quickly and hoped her vaporous heat wouldn't hurt her twin.

As Star sobbed along with Celia, her psyche flooded with memories: the preacher's hands fishing in Celia's underwear, his sweaty weight pressing her skinny bones into the mattress, his sour taste flooding her child mouth. She anchored herself in the cells of Celia's skin, riding out her sister's storm, just like she had Lake Monroe's.

CHAPTER TWENTY-TWO

The preacher was nearly as stunned by Celia's accusation as his wife had been by Star's drowning. His daughter's returned memories meant, well...death to the preacher. He clutched his pounding chest. He would do the only thing he knew how in a crisis: pray. Lifting the candle high above his bandaged head, he stumbled down the dark hall toward the sanctuary. The sound of weeping caused him to stop outside Celia's room. He put his ear against the wood panel and listened; her sobs of pain flooded his senses. Suddenly, a memory of Celia lying in her twin bed, him above, her sweet breath brushing his whiskered cheek and his knees buckled, landing him hard on the cold floor. Sobbing, he clutched at his head, pulling off the loose gauze and throwing it aside. "Help me, Lord. Please, Jesus, forgive me, God forgive me."

He wiped his eyes and nose with the sleeve of his sweater and reached a hand toward the knob, wrapping his fingers around the cold metal and pulling himself to standing. "Celia?" he said, opening the door. "Daughter, I've been praying for you."

The preacher held the candle high as he stepped into her bedroom. Shadows danced around her small form where it curled beneath the covers. "The Lord has spoken. We'll get you to a doctor."

"Go away," Celia cried.

"I'm worried about you." He set the candle on the nightstand and pulled aside the covers. Reaching beneath his daughter's neck and knees, he readied himself and tried to lift her off the bed.

Sobbing, she shoved him hard. "Leave me alone, Daddy. I hate you."

"Shhhh," he said. "It's the fever talking. If I don't get you to a doctor soon, you could end up in a stupor like your mother." He pulled at her body until he'd wrestled her against his chest like the child she was.

"Put me down." She swiped at him with her fingernails. "I'm not sick."

Knocking sounds flicked around the room, banging louder as they increased in frequency. The preacher froze. A scattering of quick taps raced across the ceiling, loudening as they centered above him. All at once, sparks of energy shot from the ceiling and light splinters stung him around his head and neck. A release of his vile memories flooded his consciousness. He dropped Celia onto the bed and swung his arms through the air, bellowing, "In God's name, be gone Satan."

Star spun her daddy in a cyclone of flashes, a twister whirling him down the hall toward the kitchen, depositing the preacher in the rocker like an armload of kindling. She left him next to the woodstove, mumbling, "My God, leave me Satan."

"It's Star, Daddy," Star whispered, and flew back through the swirls of frenetic energy to the bedroom where her feverish sister had pulled herself back beneath the covers.

"Celia," she whispered, "I took care of him. You can sleep easily now." Star laid blue filaments over Celia's forehead, pulsing light through her twin's aura.

"Star," Celia said, and fell into a deep sleep.

Celia awoke to the sound of her daddy bustling about the kitchen. Despite everything, the smell of oatmeal enticed her. She looked around the room for an alternate exit and momentarily considered fleeing, but there was only the window, and the snow had drifted against the house in the night, blocking the sill with heaps of white.

She swung her legs over the side of the bed, touching her bare feet to the cold floor. Upon standing, her fever-weakened body buckled and she dropped back onto the bed. Still the smell of food drew her. She recalled hurrying to eat brown-sugar-sprinkled mush as a kid, excited by the trip to the orchard with Daddy, who would take the twins sledding. Even as they barreled down the hill toward the orchard, Celia felt tense, wary of the darkness looming beyond the bare apple branches. She'd been afraid of her daddy all along.

"Star," she said, looking around. The light was clear and bright in the bedroom. Outside the window, snow fell steadily. Star didn't answer. She would have to face her daddy alone. She slipped on her robe, opened the bedroom door, and leaned against the doorframe. Her daddy stirred oatmeal in a big pot on the woodstove. The mush sputtered, smelling sweet with brown sugar. She raised her hands to cover her stomach, imagining somehow that their fine bones and fair skin would fortify her against her daddy's pretense.

The preacher turned. His bruised eyebrow greenish beneath the undressed and blackened stitches. His eyes were red, mouth turned down, his right eye blue-black. He looked wild and demonic. Celia grabbed the doorframe more tightly to steady herself.

He dropped the spoon in the mush pot and bolted to her side. His movement was so sudden that she crouched, fearing he might slap her, but all he did was slip a hand beneath her elbow and draw her to standing. She faced away from his smell of old wool and instant coffee as he led her to the rocker.

"I'm not sure you should be up," he said, "you've been delirious with fever."

"I can walk by myself," she said, jerking her elbow free.

"Let's get some hot cereal down you and see how you feel then. If that doesn't do the trick, I'll drive you to the doctor."

Celia took a seat in the rocker. Had he already drawn up the quitclaim? Was she to be handed over to the sanitarium along with the churchhouse? Shuddering, she realized it wasn't oatmeal she wanted, it was someone to stand beside her, someone other than her daddy scooping mush into a chipped bowl, feigning concern and protection. "I need to make a call," she said, and started to get up again.

"Sit down," he said, setting a hot bowl in her hands. Steam rose off the still-bubbling cereal and dampened her face. She felt her hunger grab her belly despite her fear. She mumbled something and leaned back in the rocker. As she settled in, her robe slipped off her legs, exposing the skin on her thighs where the scars had miraculously vanished.

The preacher's eyes fell over her perfect flesh. "My God," he said. "The miracle."

Perhaps it was the tunnel the preacher had heard about, the hallway to Jesus' Kingdom that every soul travels down once departed from flesh. That very hallway now rushed toward him, the intensity of its dark shadows and bright light felling him where he stood, barely missing the stool with his injured forehead as he toppled to the kitchen floor, oatmeal spattering.

"Daddy," Celia shrieked.

He saw nothing but a milky face surrounded by a tangle of what appeared to be writhing snakes. In his mind he tried to shout, "Enough Satan, enough!" but his mouth didn't work. Ghostly at first, the serpents darkened, coming into focus above him. As his vision cleared, he realized it was his dark daughter waving something acrid beneath his nose. The preacher jerked his head away from the sharpness, his sinuses assaulted by ammonia.

"You saw it, didn't you, Daddy?" Celia sat back on her heels, waiting out his coughing spell. "You saw the miracle and fainted."

"I lost my balance," he said, seeking her forgiveness with his eyes, wanting to say he'd done it all. Yes, all the things Celia had accused him of. He brought a hand to his forehead, rubbing his aching head. He was about to say, "Yes, the miracle," but instead he said, "My head hurts."

Celia got up slowly, disappearing somewhere behind where the preacher lay on the cold kitchen floor. Cupboard doors banged and water spilled from the kettle, hissing on the hot stove. Then Celia's voice, still faint from her fever, spoke close to his ear, "What should I do with you, Daddy? Take you to the doctor? Sign you up for a lengthy stay at the sanitarium, like you were going to do with me?"

The preacher groaned, edging his shoulders away from her, adjusting his painful hips where they pressed against the icy floor.

Celia knelt beside him. "I don't understand how you could do it—violate your own child. It's repulsive." Her violet-scented fingers pushed a pill between his lips. He pinched them tightly together and turned away.

"It's an aspirin, Daddy. What'd you think, I'm poisoning you? Now open your mouth. I'll give you a drink of water."

He swallowed. A coolness spread across his tongue, contracting his jaw. He pulled back, looking hard at Celia. There was no vehemence in those dark eyes, just deep sadness staring down at him, a sadness that he'd always blamed on her boss or a boyfriend or some one-night stand. She looked so tired. It was all his fault.

"Drink up," she said, tipping more melted snow into his mouth. "Jay's a policeman; he'll know what to do about your crime. I'll make a call after I clean up the oatmeal." She pushed a pillow beneath his head, tossed an afghan over his chilled torso, and left him lying there on the floor.

I need to get up, he thought, and leaned up on an elbow. The throbbing in his head overwhelmed him. He fell back, staring at the ceiling, studying the soot-smudged tongue and groove; it would take more than one bucket of hot soapy water to remove all the blackness. As he stared, the smudges on the white ceiling morphed into Vanessa's dark hair falling over the pleated shoulders of her white choir robe, the sheen of satin making her look more angelic than he remembered. "Vanessa?" he said.

"What, Daddy?" Celia said.

"Nothing," he said. His thoughts drifted to choir practice eons ago when Vanessa and the others joined their sweet voices together, letting them rise angelically from the church-house's sanctuary. As he closed the truck door, the beautiful sound muffled. At times, he'd sit there in the truck cab's stuffiness ready to drive away, thinking he could manage his evil desires. Despite his efforts to walk the straight and narrow, eventually the Devil took possession once again. He left the truck and crept back inside. Upstairs, he found the twins playing on their beds, their rumpled cotton pajamas dotted with pink poodles, Celia's hair a storm, Star's a circle of light. He'd sent Star outside to play, and then what happened next had awakened him in the middle of the night in a panic more times than he could count. He closed his eyes, shaking his head, clutching tightly to his denial. God's forgiveness was the only thing that would save him from Satan's incinerator.

Wood clattered to the floor. He jumped. The woodstove's cast-iron door creaked open, then the snapping and popping of a replenished flame released a puff of smoke into the room, relaxing him. He closed his eyes, forgetting, for the moment, his trespasses.

The problem with being human, Star thought, *is humans keel over at the stupidest things. Scaredy-cats, all of them, just big jumpy scaredy-cats*. Star floated above her father, noting his shocked expression. *Everyone's in shock*, she thought, *really, even the dead soldiers from the war, their spirits flying over Vinegar Valley like numb sightseers, are still aching; yes, everyone has suffered shock one time or another. Forgetting could be blissful, in a dull sort of way.*

But the afterlife comes with a set of rules, the paramount one being—you stick around the earthly plane for too long, you lose your memory and end up haunting the living for the rest of time. So, dead or alive, forgetting isn't a good idea.

Star knew that the best thing to do for amnesia was to snap the sufferer out of it—which went for all humans on either side of the veil. *Even if someone's actions are as frightening as Lake Monroe's feigned monster, waking is essential.*

Star watched the preacher resting there on the kitchen floor while her frowning sister worked steadily around him, scrubbing up bits of oatmeal from the rocker and the linoleum, gummy stuff that had flown from the bowl when he dropped his oatmeal at the sight of Celia's healed burn scars. Amazingly, the bowl remained in one piece.

Finished, Celia walked to the corner near the coat hooks to replace the broom. She bent down and picked up an envelope that had fallen from the preacher's jacket pocket. Star watched her sister study it and then raise her eyebrows, turning to where their daddy rested on the floor—a light had come on inside that darkly curled head of hers.

"The quitclaim and deed," Celia said, striding over to her father. "Goddamn you, you were actually going to go through with it."

Of course, he was, Star thought, knowing that with this information, everything would work out for Celia. Star slipped away, her molecules drifting up the stairs to her old bedroom where she'd take a little rest.

Startled, the preacher leaned up on his elbow. "Give me those," he said, reaching for the papers.

Celia held the deed and quitclaim out of reach. She folded the deed and slipped it into the envelope and inside her robe. She stepped around him, kneeling down next to him with the quitclaim in her hand. "Shame on you, Daddy," Celia said. "Now cross out Luna Sanitarium and put my name there. Initial it, Daddy. I'm putting all of this in a safe place. And we'll be done with this silliness."

"I won't sign it," he said. "Now give it to me."

"Oh, yes you will. Because I know what really happened in the orchard," she said. "And upstairs. And in the root cellar. Here's a pen. Now sign it!"

The preacher leaned up on his elbow and did as he was told. "I can get another quitclaim," he said. "Just like that."

"Yes, but I have the deed. Now get up and get dressed. We're going to visit Mama."

"But the storm...."

"The storm's nothing compared to the mess you're in. Oh, and while we're at the sanitarium, you can tell the doctor you'll be making monthly payments for Mama's stay." She turned and walked down the hall to her bedroom.

The preacher called after her, "I'll tell that cop boyfriend of yours that you're a thief."

"I guess you now know how it feels to be threatened."

Celia closed the bedroom door and opened the closet. Reaching to the back shelf, she stowed the envelope beneath a stack of blankets. She turned from the closet and dropped onto the edge of the bed, lifted the receiver, and dialed Jay. When she heard the sound of his voice, she cried, "JJ, I need to talk to you. Daddy...well, he's done something terrible."

Jay sighed, "Now what?"

"I don't want to talk about it over the phone. Will you meet me later?"

"Where?"

"Peggo's Grill?"

"Well, you're in luck. I need to eat dinner sometime. Seven?"

"Yes, thank you. I'm going to see Mama now."

"Bad conditions still," he said. "Be careful."

Celia set the receiver in the cradle and changed out of her oatmeal-stained robe into jeans and a red sweater. As she fastened her heart locket around her neck, the attic floor creaked. The sound reminded her of Star's furniture-rearranging episodes; the scraping usually took place while Celia was trying to sleep, or after a one-night stand stumbled out the front door into the thin morning light.

Celia brushed her hair, lined her eyes heavily with kohl, and applied red lipstick. When Star was alive, she never said anything about Celia's line of work. Celia knew Star disapproved, making comments once in a while about the price of silk or fine leather, even 100% *virgin* wool—like her beautiful coat that now had a big stain on the tush from falling in the road. Maybe it would come out at the cleaners, or maybe it wouldn't. Star was right, though; she liked expensive things—but hey, Celia gave her all for the boys at the club. She had worked hard for every woven thread she purchased.

Celia sprayed on Mist of Violets. She guessed the reason she was wilder than her twin was because of what had happened with Daddy. She wasn't innately rotten. The preacher had made her the way she was. "Isn't that right, Star?"

The ceiling creaked again.

"Like Mama said, I'm dark as lily roots."

The stairs groaned and for a moment, Celia thought her twin would flow through the door in a milky haze. Instead, her daddy cleared his throat.

"I'm ready," came his muffled call from the kitchen.

CHAPTER TWENTY-THREE

Vanessa sat in a wheelchair, a white afghan draped over her narrow lap. Usually her frailty shocked Celia, but today the anguish she felt over her daddy's betrayal was all-consuming. She threw her coat on the bed and took a seat next to her mother. Sighing, she said, "Mama, I brought Daddy to see you. He's on his way up the stairs now."

She picked up the lotion bottle from the bedside table and squeezed a dab onto her palm. Gently, she massaged her mother's dry hands. "I need to talk to you, Mama, about Daddy. I know you can hear me, if you would just blink your eyes to acknowledge my words, I'd be so grateful. I need your help. Please, Mama, wake up."

Star knew that Vanessa didn't hear Celia, for their mother had wandered far into the woods, singing softly to herself as she bundled sticks. Her long black hair was tied back with a white sash that matched her dress. She was pure of heart, unlike the others who faltered, the ones who stayed lost in the darkness forever.

"Mama," Star said, picking up sticks along with her. "Listen to Celia. Daddy's been keeping a secret. It's time he tells the truth."

Vanessa didn't acknowledge Star, just continued to wander beyond the veil, gathering sticks into bundles.

"Talk to her, Sissy," Star whispered. "Tell her about the storm."

"Mama," Celia said, ready to explain how her memories had returned. Even though the words pressed against the back of her teeth, she couldn't speak about what her daddy had done. "Daddy's been staying with me, Mama, because the weather's terrible. We've had feet and feet of snow. And the power's been out for days. It's been miserable."

The door flung open and the preacher walked into the room. His green sweater buttoned to the neck, his stitched forehead and fading bruise, his greasy hair; all of it looked out of character for the man of cloth. Star whooshed across the room, swirling around him, whispering, "What a lovely place to keep the insane, or the not-so-insane, like our mother. Don't you think Daddy?"

The preacher crossed the room to where his wife sat and placed his heavy hand on her thin shoulder. "Vanessa, dear. I'm here, sweetheart." He kissed her forehead.

Star watched her mother turn from the scattered twigs she was gathering. She looked toward the path. "Never go into the woods without a rifle, Edward," Vanessa said from afar. "There are wolves, you know."

Star knew her mother had been taught not to interfere in a man's affairs. But now that she was privy to the woods—the crunching underbrush, the scent of sun-heated sap—things had changed. Vanessa watched her husband from her hiding place. He left her side and ranged around the room, opening lids and capping them again: jars of cotton balls, bottles of alcohol, tongue depressors, and little red pills. He walked to the windows and stood with his hands clasped behind his back, staring out at the falling snow.

"Daddy," Celia said. "Did you talk to the doctor?"

"Not yet," he said. "I've just now arrived and greeted my sweet wife. Give me a minute."

Density of matter, Star thought, her whispers expanding and contracting with the dimming and brightening of the generator lights. *It's not spirit if it's dense, is it?*

Vanessa lifted her finger to her mouth and made eye contact with Celia.

"Mama," Celia said, grabbing her mother's hand. "Star's ashes. They're in the lake."

"Spider silk," Vanessa said.

"Star's gone," Celia said, tears streaming down her cheeks. "I'll comb your hair, Mama. Where's your lipstick? Daddy, tell the doctor Mama's awake."

"Celia!" Vanessa whispered.

Shock, the doctor called Vanessa's condition—*nothing in, nothing out—one of many mechanisms designed to protect the individual's psyche.*

The preacher had become a pro at *nothing in, nothing out*, especially when it came to sore feelings around his dark-daughter's behavior. Take for instance the day he was on his way to the food bank last summer in Etta's car and Celia was wandering around outside the club, her skirt so short that a quick breeze would have fluttered it above her waist. When he'd called her over to the borrowed car, the angry face on her was unnerving. He tried to make his presence there seem innocent, although it wasn't. He'd gone there specifically to see what she was up to; however, he didn't expect to run into her.

"I'm on my way to the food bank," he'd said. "Get in. I'll give you a ride home."

"What are you doing here, Daddy? And whose car is this?"

"A church volunteer loaned it to me," the preacher said. "The fan belt on my truck broke. Come on, get in."

"I'm waiting for Raven," she said and sashayed away. "We've got practice today," she called over her shoulder. "You know, those naughty moves we do don't come naturally."

He sat there, angrily assessing his dark daughter. Beyond her, the cold-storage building that housed the club was deteriorating like their relationship. He rolled up the window, praying as he backed the car around. Celia looked back from the stairs and flipped him off. She then disappeared inside the club. He jumped, gulping saliva as he turned the wheel and headed for the road, choking.

Now, he was practically running down the hall, bellowing the news of his wife's return. The dark-eyed maniac shuffling outside Room 340, the nurse with the stethoscope and sour demeanor, the white-haired janitor with a mop bucket, all looked startled as he flew past them. If Etta had been there, he would have spun her around like he'd done with the twins when they were children. So happy to have his wife awake, he shouted, "Doctor, doctor, my wife's awake; she's awake! Oh, thank the Lord, my Vanessa's awake."

With a whoop, the doctor rushed him, shaking his hand, clapping him on the back. "Preacher Monroe, this is exciting news. Very exciting indeed. I'll get my stethoscope."

"Yes, and about our agreement," the preacher said. "Due to some unexpected circumstances, I'll need to go back to monthly installments, rather than signing over the little churchhouse to the sanitarium."

"This is a momentous occasion, Preacher. First your wife, then business."

CHAPTER TWENTY-FOUR

Celia chuckled. She felt absolutely giddy, stirring tomato soup over the woodstove, adding sprinkles of cayenne, a little extra in her daddy's bowl as punishment for his betrayal. It wasn't Peggo's Grill, but who could complain, since less than an hour earlier she'd practically leapt from her skin when her mama opened her eyes and spoke her name.

Tomato soup wasn't on the sanitarium's menu, just Jell-O and bouillon. The chipper male attendant always smiled at Vanessa. And more than once Celia had seen him flourish a hand, like the item on the tray was some gourmet dish offered in a French restaurant, not that Vinegar Valley had ever experienced anything French, except of course, a kiss or a salty fry.

Celia left the woodstove, practically dancing as she placed a saucer of saltines on the picnic table. Next to the plate, she set a bowl of jam and dish of butter. She filled mugs with hot water and stirred honey into the black tea. Despite her daddy's attitude—*Don't get your hopes up, she might not stay awake*—Celia would celebrate her mama's awakening with gusto. She turned and called, "Daddy, time for dinner."

Sitting at the table, a bowl of soup steaming before her, Celia studied the sagging sky. Pleated clouds, gray and heavy, moved in from somewhere southwest where apples still hung on leafy trees. The valley would be swamped with melt-off in no time—water coursing through ditches, traversing roads, soaking fields. Virgin lakes would form for south-flying mallards. All that water would reflect the sodden sky.

Slippers slapped the stairs. Celia turned. The preacher stood in the doorway, his face blank, his lips narrow, obviously the notion of celebration would be lost on him. A gust of wind blasted the windows. Celia imagined Jay cruising rural roads, pulling ditch-divers back onto the shoulder. He'd have made a better dinner date than her daddy. She actually looked forward to seeing him later at Peggo's, even though her thoughts still turned to Johnny.

"I'm ready to go home," the preacher said, shuffling across the room, his bag in one hand, his Bible in the other.

Celia looked up. "Later, Daddy." Celia struck a match and held it to the candle wick. "Right now, we're celebrating Mama's awakening; since Star returned, we've had two miracles."

The preacher grumbled. "My pipes are thawing as we speak." He scratched at the black stitches poking through his eyebrow. "Whichever pipe split in the freeze will thaw by morning. I can prevent a flood if I replace the break now."

"It's just beginning to thaw, Daddy. The Chinook isn't expected to hit until after midnight." Celia lifted a spoonful of soup to her mouth, blowing on the hot liquid. "Did you talk to the doctor about the churchhouse?"

"He knows," the preacher said, quietly. He set his duffle bag by the door and shuffled to the picnic table. "And to think I could have—" He slapped the Bible down onto the table a little too loudly.

"Could have what, Daddy?" Celia said. "Rendezvoused with that woman I saw you with the other night?"

"Mrs. Etta Marcus works at the church," he said, taking a seat opposite her. "She's been a godsend to the congregation."

"Cut the bull, Daddy!"

The refrigerator clunked a couple times and rattled to life, the sound disrupting the tension building between them. Beyond her daddy, the porch light flashed on. "Smile," she said, "the power's back on."

The preacher stared at her for a few moments, and then bowed his head in prayer. Finished praying, he settled in, spooning soup into his mouth. "Ach," he said, flinching from the red pepper. Grumbling, he wiped his mouth with a napkin, giving his daughter a disgusted look.

"I'm meeting JJ at Peggo's Grill later," Celia said. "Didn't want you to miss out on the cayenne, Daddy." She buttered a cracker and licked her fingers clean. "I'll drop you at home on my way into town."

CHAPTER TWENTY-FIVE

Celia's threat to talk to the law had the preacher feeling a loss similar to Lot's. He had to own up to his bad behavior, move on from his former life. Or salt it would be! He set down the pipe wrench. Everything crammed beneath the sink was now scattered about on the floor where he crouched before the pipes. He loaded some of the stuff back under the sink and got to his feet. He stood gingerly as his legs, which had cramped while bent beneath him, felt unstable.

He knew clouds rolling in from the southwest meant a warm wind would soon be melting off the snow, and basements and kitchens and bathrooms would flood. The fittings he'd hauled from the basement had worked in the right combination, and the cracked section of the broken pipe was repaired before it had a chance to leak.

The house had gotten away from him. It would take him half the night to clean it thoroughly. He stuffed the rest of the kitchen mess into garbage bags. He hated being pushed around by church members, the board, and now his only child. He doubted Jay's involvement would help her; after all, he's a cop killer. But, if they did embark on a witch hunt—or at least make things difficult for him, he could lose his church. And his reputation. What was the point of taking someone down, anyway? If he wanted to go down, he could take a swim or a plummet off a cliff, or....

He shrugged. Either he could wallow in the swollen darkness or trust God's guidance. He thought of Etta and his groin came alive. Her imagined fragrance tickled his nose as he tied up a garbage bag laden with half-empty cleanser cans, a Spic and Span box, old rags, and several cracked vases; things Vanessa had saved. All of it had to go. And the mess on the kitchen counters and the table. He stacked several trash bags by the door and was fumbling through the broom closet for a mop bucket when he heard the front door squeak open.

"Edward, are you home?" Etta stepped into the kitchen. "You've hurt yourself." She hurried over to him, touching his forehead lightly with cool fingers.

He took her hand. "It's nothing." He smiled weakly as the scent of rose dusting powder twined around him. He knew the smell would linger on his fingers, and when later he brought them to his nose, he'd disguise the gesture as prayer. "Oh, how I've missed your casseroles; Celia loaded the soup with cayenne tonight. My lips are still burning."

"I've missed you, too." Etta smiled widely, then leaned in and kissed him on the cheek.

The weight in his legs suddenly had him immobilized. God, how he craved his hands on her breasts, his lips pressed against hers. But this was his wife's house, too. He released her hand. "I was about to mop the floor, and I have bedding to change," he said, retrieving the mop bucket. "Vanessa's coming home."

"She's awake?" Etta said, not taking her eyes off of his. Then she looked down at her shoes. "That's wonderful, Edward. I'll help with the bedding, if you like."

He imagined her perfume lingering on the sheets. "Maybe it would be best if…."

"I see what you mean," she said. "The dishes then, I'll wash them before I go." She reached to touch his stitched brow. "Does it hurt much?"

"Itches," he said, lifting the bucket of soapy water from the sink to the floor. "The stitches will come out soon." He dunked the mop in and out of the soapy water and swished it around the yellow linoleum.

Etta stepped around him to the sink and began to scrape and stack the soiled plates. "Edward," she said, her voice cracking.

The preacher straightened. "I can't, you know." He looked at his wet shoes, thinking of his reputation. He'd already made one fatal mistake; he didn't dare make another.

"When you're finished cleaning, come to my place; I'll heat leftovers," she said. "That's why I stopped by, to invite you over."

"I'll make us some tea," he said, slowly setting the mop aside. We'll sit for a moment, then I must get back to work." He put the kettle on. "Pipes break at your place?"

"I have gas appliances." Etta shrugged. "I feel a little guilty. People have been suffering so much with all the cold."

"I wish I'd known." The preacher dropped his big hands to his sides and watched the steam pour from the kettle spout. "Black tea is all we have."

"That's fine," Etta said. The powder she wore caked into the edges of her lipstick. "I'll be at the church early Sunday morning cleaning before the service." She took a seat at the table and crossed her hands in her lap. "Hot coffee will be waiting for you, as always."

"That'll be nice," he said. "God kept His watchful eyes on the church's plumbing, and the seams stayed tight. We have been blessed once again."

"I left the faucets dripping, Ed. That's what you do in a hard freeze."

"Of course." He frowned, thinking of Jay's advice as he poured boiling water into teacups. He'd seen water freeze once, an icicle from faucet to porcelain sink. It was a terrible thing. He dropped teabags into the cups. "Careful, it's hot."

He stood watching steam rise from the cups, feeling all fidgety inside. He cleared his throat, got up and pulled the curtains and switched on the nook light. Now he could see her blushing powder and green eyes, her cleavage plump beneath the lacy neckline. Leaving his tea untouched, he took her by the hand and led her to the bedroom.

"Coffee and chocolate cake," Jay said.

"Coming right up, Officer Johnson." The waitress splashed coffee into his cup then hurried off.

As Jay stirred sugar cubes into the black liquid, he eavesdropped on two old guys talking about their tractors. Something about a broken John Deere not being good for much other than the scrap heap. Jay had driven a tractor once when he was young—*young and wild*, he thought, *shooting BBs at helpless birds*.

"Tractor seat's broke all to hell," the grizzled guy said.

"Duct tape 'ill fix it," the bald guy said. "Few wraps with that, she'll be as good as new."

The bell above the door jangled. Jay pivoted on the counter stool. It was Celia. She bent forward, moving her delicate hands like bird's wings, brushing dirt from the knees of her tight jeans. She'd fallen, he guessed; the girl was sexy, but clumsy. Usually he disapproved of what she was wearing, but right now all he could do was smile as he took in the plunge of her neckline between the lapels of her open coat—she was a beauty with all that black hair and red pouty lips. *Kiss and reconsider*, he thought.

"JJ," she said, climbing onto the stool next to him. She removed her coat and kissed his cheek. "Thanks for meeting me here."

"Coffee, Miss?" the waitress said, smiling.

Celia nodded and returned the smile.

Watching the two women interact made Jay recall the moon-faced waitress he'd talked to the last time he was here. He realized he'd almost kept going that day, driving straight out of town, leaving everything behind that was familiar and perhaps even damn good. He cleared his throat and looked around the small café. Outside, he could see the wind tossing tree branches, snow-covered maples lining the street, their shadows jumping in the light of the streetlamp.

"This has been a week from Hell," Celia said. "You walked out and Daddy walked in. Then I remembered something I could have done without forever."

Jay raised his eyebrows, "Huh?"

"And get this," she said, covering her mouth with her hand. Tears filled her eyes, spilling down her cheeks. She grabbed a napkin. "Sorry," she said, dabbing her eyes. She smiled brightly. "Mama's awake."

"What?" Jay circled her shoulders with his arms. "That's the best news I've heard in a long time." He squeezed her tightly, patting her back, "Wonderful news!" he said, letting go.

Celia turned to the counter and took a sip of coffee. "Gosh, that's good. I've been gagging on instant all week."

"Uh huh, well, coffee's good here no matter what you've been drinking at home. So, what's going on, Celia?"

"You know how Daddy preaches that we obey the law? Well, he doesn't take his own advice."

"God's law, you mean?" Jay said. "I thought at first that you meant man's law."

"Well, both." She turned to look at him, eyes tearing up again. She didn't drop her eyes as she whispered, "I need to tell you about the bad thing, but I'm not sure I can."

The waitress brought a large slice of chocolate cake and set it, along with two forks, in front of Jay. He pushed a fork toward Celia then lifted his own to the dessert. He took a bite. The sweetness filled his mouth. "Hmm, have some," he said, and pushed the plate nearer Celia. "It's delicious. And...," he leaned in close, "cops use it as truth serum."

Celia smiled. She cut into the cake and took a bite.

Jay watched her closely, "You're not saying that he...?"

Nodding, Celia wiped her mouth with the napkin. "Early summer mornings...when Mama was at choir practice. He sent Star away, and then...."

"Turn him in." Jay took her hand, rubbing his thumb gently over her knuckles. "Sorry, but you know how people are. The public will be rough on you. Especially since...."

"I want him to be sorry. Really sorry!" Celia lowered her eyes.

Jay thought of Larry's wife and kids and pushed the cake away. "I'll take you over there. You'll get your apology if it kills me."

Celia sat in the passenger seat next to Jay. "Buckle up," he said, fastening his seatbelt across his lap. He wished he was shoveling a driveway in some quiet neighborhood in some far-off town, a place where Larry hadn't lived, where Celia didn't strip, where the preacher hadn't crossed the line—guys like him didn't fare well in jail. He wanted to live some place where life was simple, where he could recharge after work, sleep in on the weekends. He put the cruiser in gear and drove off down the snowy tree-lined street. Wind volleyed a clump of melting snow across the cruiser's windshield. Celia shrieked. Jay switched on the windshield wipers.

"Maybe that's what the preacher needs, a good scare," Jay said, turning onto Route 1. He picked up speed. The snow was softening, but slippery yet. He backed off, executing caution, even though he was excited, imagining tying the preacher's hands or cuffing him to a kitchen chair; a pistol whipping for deflowering a child wouldn't be out of the question—the most despicable of all crimes. Pedophiles never make it to the end of their sentences.

Next to him, Celia fidgeted. He turned to her in the low light. Her head was in her hands. She sighed heavily. There was no proof of what had happened between the two of them all those years ago, but even then, justice for the victim was important. How to get it, he wasn't sure.

Celia looked up. He wanted to protect her, but how could he when her reputation was less than perfect and her sister (had she known?) wasn't alive to testify. And that mother of hers had been sleeping like Rip van Winkle ever since Star's drowning. Even though the woman was awake now, Vanessa probably wouldn't be good for much for some time. *Lingering lethargy*, he imagined. Or even a return to shock.

He turned onto the preacher's street and parked his rig nose to nose with the old man's truck. He turned off the engine and felt for his gun. Its solid weight rested heavily against his hip, the workings of the weapon assembled carefully, perfectly sheathed in its leather holster. "Okay then, ready?" he said.

Celia nodded. They climbed from the car, stepping through the heavy snow to the preacher's front door. The air smelled like wet earth and a south wind. Knocking, Jay stepped behind Celia and waited, the warm wind whipping at their clothing and hair. A Chinook was on its way.

At last, the door opened, and the preacher stood there, his shirt loose, surprise written across his face.

"What are you two doing here?"

"I want to talk to you," Celia said, "you know...about what happened."

The preacher drew his fingers through his hair. "It's not a good time. I was about to mop the kitchen floor."

"Sir, if you don't mind, Celia has something to say to you. And from what I've heard, you owe her a listen."

"Daddy," Celia said. "Please, this is hard enough without making me stand out here in the cold. Let us come inside."

Grumbling, the preacher stepped out of the way.

Jay placed his hand on the small of Celia's back and guided her into the room. He looked around at the easy chairs strewn with clothing, the card table covered with sheets of yellow legal paper, and Bible-study books open and stacked face down in a pile. *Fuck*, he thought. *The old man's losing it.*

Celia fingered the edge of her wool coat, turning to Jay for assurance. "Daddy, you've called me a jezebel in public. You've made everyone think of me in a bad way, glare at me even. Your parishioners need to know that you made me this way. You're to blame, not me."

The preacher took a step backwards. "No one respects a stripper. You've ruined your own reputation. Like I already said, I'll let you stay in the churchhouse. Now you'd better get going. I have cleaning to do before your mother…."

"A public confession; I saw it once in a movie." Jay nodded toward Celia, who steadied herself against the card table. "Look at her, Sir. She's miserable. You can make it right. All you have to do is come clean."

The preacher clenched his fists. "I don't know why you're here. This misunderstanding is family business, not police business. Now leave." The preacher stepped forward. "Celia sees her dead sister's ghost, for Heaven's sake. Who'd believe someone so unstable? No public confession, no nothing."

"I'm not the only one who's seen Star," Celia said. "The day we picked you up, you called me Star. And then the other night by the woodstove. Twice, you've seen her!"

"I've been overly tired lately, Celia. The blizzard, your shenanigans, your mother's state of mind, the injury in the crawlspace." He rubbed his hand over his forehead.

"You've committed a crime, Sir," Jay said, feeling the billy club beneath his fingertips. "So, what's it going to be, a ride to the police station or a public confession?"

The preacher looked toward the bedroom door and back. "I already apologized," he said. "Now get out of here, I need to clean house. And I have a sermon to write." He grabbed Celia by the shoulders and pushed her toward the door.

"Daddy, I'm not leaving," Celia said, shaking him off. "The confession's a good idea. You need to pay for what you did."

"I've already paid," he shouted, raising his hands as if to strike his dark daughter. "The Devil has seen to that."

Jay grabbed the preacher's wrists and backed him into the easy chair. "Haven't you done enough damage," he shouted. "This Sunday," he said, heatedly. "A public confession, you hear?"

"It'll be the ruin of me. And poor Vanessa. She's been through enough," the preacher said, glancing at the bedroom door again.

"What's in the bedroom, Sir?" Jay started across the room.

"Wait. It's a shambles. I sign her out tomorrow, you know that. I haven't finished...."

Jay looked into the room. Piles of bedding and dirty clothes were scattered everywhere. He turned back. "A mess, all right. Ready to go Ceal?" he said.

Celia nodded. "I'll be sitting in the front pew, Daddy."

The preacher stood at the kitchen window watching the patrol car drive off. It stopped at the corner, turn signal blinking and then turned right, red taillights disappearing around the bend.

He knew that a confession would be a death sentence. He turned away from the window and walked through the kitchen to the bedroom. It smelled of rose dusting powder, just as he had feared. Etta sat on the end of the bed, worrying her buttons with her fingers.

"I hid behind the bed," she said. "What was he talking about?"

"It's all a mistake," the preacher said, taking a seat next to her. He petted her hand, staring at the button she'd missed.

She brought her hands to her chest and buttoned the last button. "Have you been stealing from the offering plate, Edward?"

"I wouldn't do that," he said, taking a hand and kissing each of her fingers. "That hoodlum; I warned Celia he was all wrong for her. He killed a man once. Did you know that?"

"I didn't even see who it was, Ed," she said, wringing her hands. "I was scared to death. Now tell me the truth…what did you do?"

"I'm handling it, Etta." He knew she'd find out sooner or later, but having her part of the congregation while he confessed would be too much to deal with. "Trust me, sweetheart; there's something I need to take care of at church Sunday. Better if you stay home." He drew the back of his fingers down her cheek. "Now, where were we?"

Etta stood. "The bed needs to be made up fresh," she said, smoothing the covers. "How can you sleep with her knowing you've been with me between these sheets?"

"Your house then?" the preacher said. "You're so beautiful; do you know that?"

Etta studied him, her pink cheeks pale in the overhead light. "I'm fooling myself. You'll never leave her."

"I've never considered leaving her, I just didn't think she'd wake up. But enough about that." He reached for the buttons on her blouse.

Etta slapped his hand away. "I'd better go," she said. "I'll come by with a casserole tomorrow afternoon. Then you can tell Vanessa and me together what you did."

CHAPTER TWENTY-SIX

Celia knew that courage didn't come naturally. Like diving into cold water, you just had to do it, not think about it. She chewed a fingernail as she turned into the Toi Toy Club's parking lot. Only part of the lot had been plowed. The club would be open that night for business. Dan better get busy.

Celia shoved through the club's side door. The wind caught it, slamming the door behind her as she stepped into the dimly lit hallway. After the freshness of the outside air, the smell of beer and cigarettes almost made her retch. Dan barreled around the corner from the music-thumping lounge, his balding head beaded with sweat, a Camel dangling from his chapped lips. "Well I'll be a mother dog, if it ain't the little starlet," Dan laughed. "Lucky for you the roads were impassable; otherwise your ass would be candy."

"You don't fool me, Dan," Celia said. "I know you love me."

Shrugging, Dan took a hard pull off his stubby cigarette. "You had your holiday, Doll," he said, leaning his head back, blowing smoke toward the ceiling. "Time to get to work; those fuckers better toss back multiple shots tonight, or… hey, where're the others?"

Celia unbuttoned her winter coat and took a deep breath. "I don't know," she said, running a hand across her damp upper lip. "Sorry, Dan. I'm not here to practice. I've come to resign. Mama's awake."

Dan tossed the smoking butt on the floor and ground it beneath his tennis shoe. "Too much holiday. It's made you lazy," he said, and tipped up her chin with nicotine stained fingers. "Work'll do you good. Now, get out of those jeans. I'll put on the whirligig music."

"No, Dan. I've decided to do something different with my life, something less smutty."

"Smutty, humph!" Dan hacked several times into his fist. "Don't kid yourself, Doll. You'll never outrun your soiled reputation."

Celia swallowed over the lump forming in her throat. "I have a hunch things will be changing real soon."

Dan lit another cigarette and shook out the match. He studied her with narrowed eyes as smoke leaked from his nostrils. "Never could get your ass here on time. Go on then; clean out your goddamned locker. I'll pull down the poster, if somebody hasn't already." Shaking his head, he took a deep pull off his cigarette and strode off.

The dressing room was just as the girls had left it the night of Star's celebration: empties cluttering the makeup counter, clothing slung over open lockers, spikes, stockings, and sweat-stained towels scattered around the room. Celia rescued the twins' picture from behind a cluster of beer bottles. She touched Star's smiling face. "Thanks, Sissy. You gave me back my life," she said, slipping the picture into her purse.

She opened the makeup drawer and removed eye shadow, liner, blush, scar cover-up, baby oil, false eyelashes, and pole glide. Piling the loot along the counter for the girls to glean, she turned to her locker. Along with sweats, leg warmers, and music cassettes, her stilettos and knee-high boots, she filled two brown bags to overflowing. She'd take the items with her. The costumes she left on the counter next to the makeup, along with a note: *Help yourself, Dolls! Your friend, Celia.*

Celia was peeling the pictures of half-naked Las Vegas dancers off the mirror when she noticed her tired reflection. She fluffed her black curls and thought about dabbing on *Rascal Red* lipstick, when she caught movement in the doorway behind her. She turned. "Dan?" Celia waited, listening, remembering the last time she'd danced, she'd gotten spooked by the footsteps she thought she heard coming down the hall. It had only been the storm blowing in, creaking the old building.

"Sissy," Star whispered. "About time you ditched this nasty place."

"Star, is that you?"

"I'm proud of you, Sissy."

Celia felt a chill waft past. She sneezed. "Star?"

Dan ducked his head around the doorframe, "Talking to yourself again, Doll?"

"Actually," Celia said, grabbing up the bags, "I wanted you to know I'm leaving this stuff here on the counter for the girls."

Dan drew his mouth sideways. "You're a strange one, girlie." He hacked against his sleeve and continued on. "You'll need this." He jammed an envelope into her hands. "Paycheck, plus a small severance." Dan slapped the doorframe and disappeared down the hall.

Back at home, wind rattled the attic window, leaking fresh air between the chinks of loose caulking. The day was furiously warm in comparison to the cold snap the valley had just survived. As Celia pulled the covers off the bed, she could smell her daddy's scent and a rush of revulsion swept over her. She tossed the sheets down the stairs, tugging down cobwebs as they tumbled through the air. "He'll be telling Vinegar Valley the truth tomorrow," she said, watching soot-covered webs spin, reminding Celia of the dancers doing the whirligig around the dance poles at the club. Despite her resolve to move on, she would miss being on stage with her friends.

She moved to the bookshelf and began packing Star's special things: yearbooks scrawled with *stay the same always*, photo albums, and the twins' baby book with a blonde and black curl taped side by side, all went into a separate box she'd save for Mama. It still seemed unreal to her that Daddy was bringing her mama home later that day. She set Star's Bible on top of the items and left the box beside the bed. She couldn't wait to visit her after church. Her stomach tightened at the thought of the confession. *Maybe it's a bad idea. Maybe I should call it off.*

She moved the remainder of the boxes under the eaves, stacking them away from the loose boards covering fluffy gray insulation, recalling the preacher's warning—steer clear of the uncovered joists—but the twins would sneak bits of fluff anyway, making doll beds in oatmeal containers on Saturday mornings while the preacher was writing his sermon. At Vanessa's prodding, he'd cut plywood to cover the insulation so the children wouldn't fall through to the kitchen below.

Celia took one last look at the rafters, lit now with the low rays of winter shining through the window, dust motes brightening as they swirled through the air. The room looked lonely with the bed stripped bare and every trace of Star's stuff packed away. She switched off the light and headed downstairs.

CHAPTER TWENTY-SEVEN

The preacher's truck bounced across the washout between the highway and Rita Road. Most of the roads were clear, with the exception of side roads, some blocked entirely by berms piled high from passing plows. Already pastures were melting into lakes. The rivers were rising and soon rushing water would be cutting across fields, flooding neighborhoods and graveyards.

He knew his life was vulnerable in the same way that loose dirt was to rushing water, and once the congregation learned of what he'd done to Celia, his position would be eroded beyond repair. And what was it that Celia said she'd dreamed? Something about Star sneaking up the stairs one day after he'd sent her outside to play. She'd witnessed the whole thing. True or not, shame washed through him at the thought of his golden child witnessing his bare ass moving on top her twin.

Shivering, he lowered the visor to block the sun's glare. *God expects a confession*, he thought, *even if Celia hadn't demanded one*.

He cracked the window, breathing in the freshness. It had been a long time since Vanessa had slept at his side, her soft snoring waking him some nights. He'd spent the night praying, asking for God's guidance as to how to handle Sunday's service. He wanted to say enough to satisfy Celia, but not so much that his career would topple. And then there was Vanessa. *I'll keep her home*, he thought. *Would Etta really show up with a casserole like she promised?* He shifted his weight on the bouncing truck seat. He'd deal with all that later.

A gust buffeted the truck sideways onto the soft sloppy shoulder, the front tire bouncing into a pothole, spraying water over the windshield. Switching on the wipers, the preacher swerved dangerously close to the flooded ditch, overcorrected, got control of the truck and barreled on. There were other options for him—the leak in the exhaust manifold, for one. But that'd send him to the burner for sure. The preacher respected a man who took responsibility for his life. Whether he would be responsible or not, he wasn't yet sure.

He slowed the truck, turning sharply to plow through the snow berm onto Luna Lake Road. Slush volleyed over the cab, the loud thuds causing him to jump despite himself. *The guards to Heaven are there*, he thought. *You just have to know how to get past them*. Another clump of snow sprayed across the truck hood. His heart sped along with the engine. Downshifting, the truck whined loudly.

Running could be his best bet. To the north, rivers were rising. He could turn around now, grab some clothes and his shaving kit and head for Canada. The draft dodgers did it, and he could too. The road wouldn't wash out completely until after he crossed the border. He'd be set. Already, Chinook winds were blowing, but not full force until later in the day. Still, he could go to church, skim over the confession, enough truth to humor her but not upset his flock. After all, Celia's appetites were inappropriate, and the townsfolk knew her behavior had nothing to do with him, a man of cloth, for God's sake.

He looked out his side window, gazing down at Luna Lake. The snow had melted around its edges, slumping into the depression in the low spot far below the hilltop where the sanitarium loomed. The truck dropped into a hole. The preacher pressed hard on the gas. The back wheels spun, fishtailing the rig. He realized he'd have to make a run for it if he wanted to get up the hill. He jammed on the brakes, but nothing happened. He punched the brake pedal over and over again. Nothing. The truck began rolling backwards, picking up speed. He pulled hard on the emergency brake. Nothing. He swung an arm over the bench seat and looked behind to steer as the truck careened downhill. The vehicle gained momentum. He decided to swing the rig around at the corner, plowing backwards into the snow piled into a high berm. Like a run-away ramp along a steep grade, the snow would stop his momentum.

Heart racing, muttering *Lord protect me* as he careened backwards down the snowy road, he turned the wheel, cornering sharply, hitting the snowbank with the full force of the truck's speed. Instead of stopping, the truck plowed through the snow berm to the other side, the bed of the truck dropping over the embankment. The preacher pitched forward, banging his head against the steering wheel. He shrieked with pain. The truck settled. He moved to unbuckle his belt and climb out, just as the rig dropped again. "Goddammit!" he shouted. Holding tightly to the steering wheel, the preacher muttered an urgent prayer as the truck plummeted through space toward the lake far below. Stomach jumping into his throat, the preacher reached for the door, ready to bail out, hit the snowy hillside and roll to safety. The door was locked. He reached for the lock just as the truck struck a rocky outcrop. The preacher's head snapped back, then whipped sideways, breaking out the side window with the impact. Everything flooded black.

The preacher's mind took on the clearness of the light at the horizon after the sun has set, color fading and darkness edging in from above. The hillsides, the trees, the lake, the orchard, all of it disappeared into the shadows. Beside him, a gauzy presence shimmered. He knew this not by looking, as his actual eyes didn't work now, but by sensing the radiance that permeated the truck cab. A feeling of complete and total love filled the preacher. All of his cells expanded, opening to love's abundance. He felt refreshed, like after a spring rain; like a newly blooming flower dotted with water droplets. Then a flash of blinding light. He lifted, or thought he lifted, his hand to shade his eyes. But his eyes weren't seeing. In fact, he no longer had a sense of his broken body. Then, in what seemed to be his imagination, one by one, fireflies lit all around him. *But there are no fireflies in Vinegar Valley. Back east somewhere, wasn't it?* Bright pinpoints of light hovered in his mind, like insects swarming on a warm summer night. And then a voice, calm and soothing said *peace* or something like that.

"Daddy?"

"Yes, Star."

"We're together again."

"Am I dead?"

"Daddy, hold my hand."

"Star? Where's Celia?"

"With Jay."

"Thank God." The lights dimmed and darkness seeped in around the preacher. Everything began to burn.

CHAPTER TWENTY-EIGHT

The Chinook howled around the corners of Vinegar Valley Bible Church, flinging the door open as each parishioner walked into the sanctuary. The smell of Chinook carried a high desert scent within the fibers of the churchgoers' wool coats and rubber boots. Celia wished to be someplace south basking in the sun instead of readying herself for a real burn. She stayed close to Raven as they entered the church.

Mostly folks walked past them without saying hello or glanced briefly and then turned away. Apparently her daddy was right, topless dancers were contagious. However, the way she figured it, if there was something to catch, it was her daddy passing it around, not her.

She removed her coat, smoothing the back of her black thrift shop dress where it clung to her thighs. Raven followed close at her heels, her strappy stilettos pecking the floor as she strutted along, her navy-blue suit looking professional although somewhat out of place. They'd shopped together, finding just the right outfits for the occasion at Easy Come, Easy Go. Raven said she'd make hers into a sexy secretary costume once she got *this nasty hubbub over with.*

They took a seat in the front row. Raven bent close, whispering in Celia's ear. "Small crowd, your Daddy may be tellin' his story twice."

Celia looked around the room. "Maybe three times."

Sun flooded through the square panes of colored glass, drenching the altar in tinted light. The horror of Celia's memories continued to reveal themselves, flowing through her body like poison. Her hands were clenched so tightly together that her knuckles had turned white. She scooted sideways, reaching her hands into the colored light that now washed over the entire front pew.

Raven's big hand enveloped Celia's icy grip. "Miss Celia?" Raven said, giving her a warm squeeze. "You sure do look like a goodie-girl in that black dress."

Celia giggled. "I didn't want to give them the satisfaction…."

"This is all I'm changin' for them tight asses," Raven whispered.

"Blue looks nice on you," Celia said, winking. She knew that decency didn't have anything to do with how one dressed; after all, her daddy would be whooshing through the side door any minute, wearing a black robe and white satin stole over his best black suit. Celia nodded toward the stage door. "Daddy should be coming through that door any second now."

"Can't wait to give him the stink-eye," Raven said.

It was the first service Celia'd been to in a long time. And due to the subject matter, it may be her last. After all, what kind of God would let bad things happen to the innocent, then let the perpetrator remain in charge? Jesus stared down at her from the gilded frame hanging above the altar. His soft brown eyes were comforting. He knew what she'd done and what had been done to her, and He loved her anyway. She relaxed a little with that knowledge.

Raven leaned close and whispered, "Where's the preacher?"

Celia turned, looking toward the back of the congregation. "Cold feet? I don't know. He better show."

The door opened and in stepped Jay, complete with uniform.

Celia's heart jumped. She raised her hand and gave him a little wave. He nodded and started up the aisle.

For a moment she imagined he'd come to arrest Daddy. But Daddy had agreed to confess, then live his life like she'd been living hers…the subject of dirty looks, nasty remarks, and people's wrath. *He'll be blackballed*, she thought. *He'll have to find other work, yes, but at least he won't spend the rest of his life in jail.*

Jay looked tense. His face seemed to say something that she couldn't quite decipher. He was worried, yes, that was it, worried. He slipped in next to her and leaned close. "How you holding up?"

"Okay. Just wondering what happened to Daddy," Celia said, biting a fingernail. "I want to get this thing over and done with! And I want to see Mama."

He nodded. "There's something you need to know. Would you step outside with me?"

EPILOGUE

Celia and her mama had been living together since her daddy's accident. Now, with full-on August heat, her Mama still spoke little. Celia didn't mind her silence, although she worried about her going into shock again. She liked to check on her between errands, as she cooked dinner, cleaned the churchhouse, or worked in the orchard, to make sure her mama was okay.

Vanessa took daily walks around the yard. Celia stood at the window, rolling Jay's engagement ring around her finger as she watched her mama wander toward the lake. Sometimes Mama stood still, staring out at nothing. Or what seemed like nothing to Celia. Maybe she was watching heat rise off the rowboat or lift from the giant lily pads. Or maybe she was looking inside her head, wandering beyond the veil, perhaps visiting with Celia's twin sister, Star.

The weather forecaster said that Vinegar Valley was suffering a drought. It seemed impossible after such a terrible winter and soggy spring. The violets were withered, which was sad. And the reeds along the lake shallows had prematurely sprouted fluff. But despite the heat, Celia was certain that everything was carrying on as planned.

At night, she and her mama dreamed together, recognizing each other beyond the veil, reaching for each other's hands. Celia always thought of it as the Unknown Place, where people who were scared of life practiced living. She would tell Mama over morning coffee how she'd seen Daddy or Star in her dreams. "Star's a bright golden orb. Daddy's still flickering. He's trying, I think."

Vanessa always nodded. "I see them sometimes, too."

On Sundays, Mama sang at church. That's when she seemed most free of her bone pain, and back to her old self.

And afterwards, at coffee hour, she chatted lightly, smiling on occasion.

Celia followed the Monroe family tradition—first the miracle, then presiding before the congregation Sunday mornings, talking about compassion, forgiveness, the nature of spirit, and of miracles. The church on Sundays was overflowing with townsfolk. Everyone nodded and said hello, often praising Celia for her helpful point of view.

Everything in Vinegar Valley carried on, even the old orchard began to thrive again.

ACKNOWLEDGMENTS

Much thanks to Jessica Stone at Penchant Press International, who walked me through the book-making process with graciousness and confidence, and to the behind-the-scene editors and designers: Lisa Dailey and Andrew Shattuck McBride, who helped make *Celia's Heaven* a beautiful book. Much gratitude to my writing buddies: Brenda Miller, Katie Humes, Rae Ellen Lee, Anita Boyle, Jim Bertolino, Susan Erickson, C.J. Prince, Carla Shafer, Kelli Russell Agodon, Annette Spaulding-Convy, and Jennifer Culkin, who gave me continued support and encouragement as I continued writing and completed this heartfelt story.

Profound thanks to my mentors Ann Pancake and Judith Kitchen (R.I.P), without whom this book may have never existed. Thanks to my fiction compatriots at PLU: Jay Bates, Julie Case, Joanna Laubscher, and Margie Lukas for thorough critiques and knowledgeable feedback. Thanks also to Centrum and Whitely Center for writing retreats—long hours of silence, conducive to clear thinking for completing the story. And thanks to The Kangaroo House on Orcas Island, and poet Jill Johnson, for the great food and shared companionship during my Artsmith Fellowship.

And much love and thanks to my family members who've supported my writing projects and artistic ventures from the get-go. To my husband, profound gratitude for all the brainstorming, reading, design suggestions, and the wealth of trivia you are always willing to share.

ABOUT THE AUTHOR

Nancy Canyon is the author of *Dark Forest* and *Saltwater* and forthcoming from Two Sylvias Press: *The Daily Artist: Day-By-Day Art Prompts for Your Practice*. *Celia's Heaven* won The Cygnus Award for Paranormal Fiction from Chanticleer Book Reviews. Ms. Canyon holds the MFA in Creative Writing from Pacific Lutheran University. She teaches and coaches for Chuckanut Writers and The Narrative Project, and paints in her Historic Fairhaven art studio. She lives in Bellingham, Washington, with her husband and two pets.